*M*ama ... sun ... occasionally snow, seeking their recipients. Sue is easy to find. Her bird sees her and spirals down to the heat of midsummer.

When Sue hears Lightning whinny outside the kitchen window, she flies out the side door of the house, looking a bit like a bird herself. Lightning doesn't talk unless he has something to say, so she assumes whatever's going on has to be important.

Something that looks like a bird is hanging out of Lightning's mouth. When she takes it and wipes the horse spit off, she sees it's addressed to her, Slewfoot Sue.

She doesn't get many letters. This is exciting.

8/11

To Sebastian

Penny Blubaugh

Serendipity

Market

Tell
your story!

LAURA GERINGER BOOKS

HARPER TEEN

An Imprint of HarperCollins Publishers

Penny Blubaugh

HarperTeen is an imprint of HarperCollins Publishers.

Serendipity Market
Copyright © 2009 by Penny Blubaugh

Library of Congress Cataloging-in-Publication Data
Blubaugh, Penny.
  Serendipity Market / by Penny Blubaugh. — 1st ed.
    p. cm.
  "Laura Geringer books."
  Summary: When the world begins to seem unbalanced, Mama Inez calls ten
storytellers to the Serendipity Market, and through the power of their magical
tales, the balance of the world is corrected once again.
  ISBN 978-0-06-146877-3
  [1. Fairy tales. 2. Storytelling—Fiction. 3. Characters in literature—Fiction.
4. Magic—Fiction. I. Title.
PZ8.B624Se 2009   2008010187
[Fic]—dc22   CIP
                                                                        AC

Typography by Jennifer Rozbruch
11 12 13 14 15   LP/CW   10 9 8 7 6 5 4 3 2 1
❖
First paperback edition, 2011

To Ron Koertge
for mentoring, friendship, and more poetry
than I could have imagined

Balance (bal'-uns) *v.* 1. To be in equilibrium. 2. To tilt, and return to equilibrium.

Spin (spin) *v.* 1. To rotate, or cause to rotate swiftly; twirl. 2. To move through the air with a revolving motion.

Contents

Sometimes it's the way a leaf tumbles to the ground. Sometimes it's the slant of the afternoon sun, or the way the moon shadows ring the rocks at the water's edge. This time it's the appearance of a yellow-green finch in March. Stories are all around, so Mama Inez and Toby always watch for signs. When Roberto sees story signs everywhere, he moans, "How will I ever learn which ones to follow?"

Toby taps Roberto's foot with his big dog paw, and Mama Inez says, "You'll know. You have gatherer blood," and Roberto has to be content with that.

Toby and Mama Inez try to follow all the signs and to slip into all the stories they can find. "Because then," Mama Inez explains to Roberto and to Franz after dinner, "when we need to balance the world, we know what stories we have to draw from, what matches, what fits." She remembers when the finch led them south and Toby became a finch, too, a chocolate-brown one. A burgundy oak leaf took them east to a puppet play with singing frogs, and Mama Inez joined the chorus. Ice crystals dangled from the moon and led to a northern kayak race.

Now Mama Inez pulls a fruit crumble from the oven and sets it to cool in front of Roberto.

Roberto, eyes on the dessert, says, "Know

what's available. That, at least, makes sense."

"So," Franz says as he slices the crumble into fourths, "maybe you should tell him just how to become a cloud, or an unobtrusive squirrel. Milk?" he adds, raising an eyebrow at Roberto.

"Yes, please," Roberto says, to both the milk and the problem of how to become a cloud.

"Oh, he already knows," Mama Inez says as she takes her share of crumble.

"Ah." Roberto sighs. "Magic. Of course . . ."

Toby, who's also having milk on his crumble, licks at his bowl with enthusiasm while Mama Inez smiles and echoes Roberto. "Of course."

How It Begins

*T*oby's bark is rough and deep. It wakes Mama Inez the same way his tongue would, if he were to lick her on the face. Sandpaper on her soul. She sits up in bed and looks outside, careful to check each cardinal direction. Mama Inez's bed is at the end of the world, on the top of the house with the witch's-hat roof. The windows look north and south, east and west. And even though the sky is a clear, translucent blue, even though the gold glimmers of sunrise still lie on the edge of the sky, she can tell that Toby is right. The spin of the world is off again.

Toby is always the first to feel it and, she supposes, she's the second, although now that Roberto's getting older, now that his powers are growing, it isn't always easy to know. Maybe this time he's the second. Still, she knows she and Toby are right.

Mama Inez pulls and twists at her thick mane of hair, lifts it off her neck, and piles it on the top of her head. She swings her legs out of bed and rubs her toes in Toby's dark coconut-shell fur. She says, "Time to get to work, then, my boy," and Toby barks once, in agreement.

Her long nightgown swirls around her ankles as Mama Inez pads across the cool morning floor. Toby follows, placing his big paws on either side of her right foot. They walk in lockstep to the old walnut desk under the east window. Mama Inez lifts the top, folds down the writing surface, sits in the smooth cedar chair, and takes out ten small envelopes shaped like birds of prey, ten pieces of paper the colors of the rainbow. She picks up a thick-nibbed fountain pen. In wide strokes she writes, ten times, "You're invited to the Serendipity Market at the end of the world. Saturday next. Bring your story, bring a talisman. Help us balance the world's spin."

She folds each invitation to fit, neatly, squarely, into the confines of the bird envelopes. Toby breathes on each letter, breathes until the wings begin to move. They're sluggish at first, but soon the birds are circling the witch's-hat tower. Mama Inez sends them on their way, kestrels to the south, hawks to the north, falcons to the west, owls to the east. Two birds each to the south and the north, three each to the west and the east.

Once the birds are gone, Mama Inez puts on her favorite black clothes and decorates them with her red scarf, the one covered with tiny mirrors that glint in the sun like snapping eyes. Then she brushes Toby until the gloss on his fur shines.

Together they begin the walk downstairs, turning in the continuous spiral that starts at the witch's-hat roof and ends at the very bottom of the house. Toby always walks down on the right, just as he always comes up on the left. Toby prefers the wide side of the stairs.

"One," murmurs Mama Inez as she begins the walk. There are sixty-seven steps, twenty-two for each floor, with one step added at the bottom, as an afterthought. Because of that trickery with the bottom step, and because she lives in a house at the end of the world where magic occurs on a regular basis, Mama Inez likes to keep track of things. She starts her day keeping track of those steps. "Sixty-seven," she says, satisfied, as her feet touch the smooth, square tiles that make the floor look as if it's built of river mud.

Her bare feet make no noise as she crosses to the kitchen. Beside her, Toby walks, and his nails click on the tiles. His feet sound like tap-dancing spiders.

Franz and Roberto look up from a breakfast of yogurt drenched in wildflower honey, and thick slices of dark brown bread. Mama Inez reaches for the teapot, pours a cup, sips it, and sighs, pleased with the warmth.

"Time for a gathering," she says.

Roberto grins at his uncle. "Ha!" he says in triumph. "I told you I felt something."

"You're always way ahead of me," Franz

says, shrugging. "You all are. I never know until the last minute, and then I have to work like the Furies to get ready."

"That's why you have me," says Roberto. "So you only have to work like one Fury, not the whole lot of them."

Franz laughs. Mama Inez looks at Roberto and says, "When you're ready, you'll be able to choose."

"Are the invitations gone?" Franz asks.

Mama Inez nods. "Saturday next," she says, speaking through a bite of bread. "Ten invitations."

"Will they all come, do you think?" asks Roberto. "Last time we just had seven. The only reason we balanced was because of the phase of the moon. I think that's why we need a gathering again so soon."

Toby barks as if he's saying yes.

There's a moment of quiet contemplation, and then Franz says, "Saturday next, you say?"

Mama Inez nods.

"Start today, Roberto?"

"Of course. Or we'll look like those Furies for real."

Franz laughs again.

Mama Inez watches them go out to their workshop, near the back of the garden, to begin planning the rings, each a token of remembrance for a storyteller. Then she and Toby go back up the sixty-seven stairs to begin some planning of their own.

Mama Inez opens a door between the west and the north windows. She's greeted by the smell of damp earth. A potter's wheel sits square in the middle of the room, surrounded by shelves of squat, sun-glazed jars. Each jar is unique in shape, in size, in color. Some are made of red river clay, some of the purple clay found beneath the willows. A few are yellow or a creamy beige, variations in the clay found in the small cave behind the waterfall that reflects the morning sun in water ribbons the color of rain.

Toby walks to each of the three bags of clay stored in this cool, damp place. He examines each bag, sniffing with his round black nose. He stops by the bag with the purple willow clay and rests a large paw against it.

"Purple, hmm?" says Mama Inez.

Toby barks once, emphatically, smiles a dog smile at her, settles down next to the bag, and closes his eyes.

Mama Inez studies the jars on the shelves. She takes down the two purple ones, takes them back into her room, and weighs them, one in each hand. She is a scale of justice, judging her jars. She looks at the jar in her right hand and shakes her head. "No. Too small for this large a stumble." Then she examines the jar in her right hand and blows out a small puff of air. "And this one doesn't have enough character."

She goes back to the potter's room and takes a thick lump of clay out of the bag. She drops it on the wheel with a smack that echoes off the wall.

"For this gathering, we need an extra-special Storie Jar," she tells Toby. Humming something that sounds like the sun glistening off water, Mama Inez begins to smooth the purple willow clay.

In the workroom by the garden, Franz and Roberto examine slices of silver and chunks of gold. They lift pieces, feel their weights, hold them up to the sky, and explore their shine.

"Peaks and valleys," Roberto says about one piece of gold.

"Filigrees," Franz answers, holding out a thick silver piece. "And look. Naughts and crosses."

"Do you think so?" Roberto says as he reaches for the piece of metal. He holds it up, lets it flare in the sun. "Well, maybe," he says after a moment. "I thought, at first, that I saw swirls. You know. Vortexes."

"And now?"

"And now I could see it going either way."

"Metals work that way," Franz agrees in a peaceful voice, and they move on to a piece of rose gold.

*M*ama Inez's birds fly through sun and wind, rain, and even occasionally snow, seeking their recipients. Sue is easy to find. Her bird sees her and spirals down to the heat of midsummer.

When Sue hears Lightning whinny outside the kitchen window, she flies out the side door of the house, looking a bit like a bird herself. Lightning doesn't talk unless he has something to say, so she assumes whatever's going on has to be important.

Something that looks like a bird is hanging out of Lightning's mouth. When she takes it and wipes the horse spit off, she sees it's addressed to her, Slewfoot Sue.

She doesn't get many letters. This is exciting.

"Bill!" Sue yells out. "Come look at what Lightning done caught."

Bill comes around the side of the house. He's red in the face and tired-looking from working outside on a day this warm, but he perks up when he sees Sue's soggy letter.

"Something good?" he asks.

"Something for me," she says, proud.

Bill looks at her. He waits, eyes wide open, while Sue turns the letter over and over, feeling the paper, looking at her name in fine script. Bill finally says, "So, what's it say?"

"Well, that's a right reasonable question," Sue says, and she opens it. But when she's done reading, Sue is still confused. "Tell my story?" she says to Bill. "Balance the spin of the world?" she asks Lightning. "Not much that's happened to me is all that unusual."

Lightning whinnies long and low, and Bill says, "Why, Sue, what about how we met? And courted? Story like that'd put most anything right." Lightning butts Sue with his big head, seeming to agree. Sue stands in the hot, hot afternoon, watches the grass ripple in the breeze, and finds that she agrees, too.

She shows both Bill and Lightning the letter one more time. She points to "Saturday next" and says, "You think I can get there by this here day? All the way to the end of the world?"

Bill laughs, pats Lightning, and says, "You and Lightning just go on ahead. Won't be no problem at all," and Lightning stomps his right front hoof three times.

Sue sends her bird back up with a "yes" written on it and starts to plan what she and Lightning will need for a trip to the end of the world and back again.

Just before she leaves, Sue says to Bill, "Wish you could come, too."

Bill hugs her hard and says, "Got to bring the herd in. You know that. But you and Lightning"—and he pats the horse—"you two'll do just fine."

❦❦

And so it goes as the world stutter-steps in its spin, as Roberto and Franz analyze pieces of metal, scrying for inspiration, as Toby and Mama Inez prepare for another gathering at the Serendipity Market.

❦❦

Tris hands Zola an envelope shaped like a falcon and waits patiently while he reads the letter inside. Whatever it is makes Zola happy, because he grins and nods his head.

"Want to share?" Tris asks.

"Nothing much." Zola's voice is light and airy. "Just an invitation to balance the world."

Tris smiles. "Should be right up your alley."

Zola stops pretending indifference and laughs, pleased and apprehensive at the same time.

❦❦

Maddie jumps up and down, excited and feeling important, when she and Earl receive their owl.

❦❦

Renata opens the second falcon and thinks of Clarisse, a wistful thought. She thinks she can't do this, not without her. But when she shows Michael the letter, he says, "You've got to go. She'd want you to be there."

Rosey and B.J., miles apart and with completely different stories, open the other two owls that have flown to the east. Both look at the invitations in surprise. Rosey fingers the paper. "It's from Gram," she says to Samson, the red bird who's stayed with her since her adventure. "But she must remember that it was a little, personal thing. Not something involved enough to fix the world."

Samson twitters, and Rosey knows it's his way of saying that Gram knows what she knows and if she wants Rosey, then Rosey should be there.

At the same time that Samson is telling Rosey to go to the end of the world, B.J. says, "Would you go?" to Nodia.

Nodia nods and says, simply, "Magic. Of course I'd go."

In the northern village of Enlay, John rolls a cigarette and looks at the hawk letter resting, wings still, on the bench. Christobel takes a furtive swipe at the letter with her claw, the hawk beak snaps, and Christobel jumps back and complains with a loud meow. John narrows his eyes and says, "Stay or go?" to Christobel or whomever else might be listening. Christobel licks a paw, acting quite unconcerned, but overhead a cloud, in a shape that mimics the hawk letter, skims over the sun. When John looks up, the cloud flaps its wings once, then disappears, which makes John say, "I take that as a yes."

Maisie gets her letter as she and Thom are starting to eat the deep-red grapes and the small round of cheese they've brought for their picnic. As the hawk wings stop moving, she opens the envelope, unfolds the letter, reads, then hands it to Thom. He reads, too, then says, "An interesting opportunity." Maisie takes three grapes, chews, then says, "I certainly think so."

❖

The kestrel wings over the Immigrant Bridge and flutters down Mae's chimney. She picks it up from the hearthstone, reads the letter, then sighs, a sigh that carries through the house, that taps against the walls. She picks up a pen and writes, "I'm so sorry. I'm on my way to my brother and sister-in-law and their almost-here baby. Should you need me at a later date (and let's hope you won't need to balance the spin again for a long, long time!), please let me know." She folds the letter, slides it into the kestrel envelope, breathes her breath on it to bring back its life, and sends it back up the chimney.

❖

From the house at the end of the world, Mama Inez and Toby watch for their birds to return. They gaze at the sky when they're hanging laundry to dry in the sun and the wind that's touched penguins and polar bears. They watch when they're gathering lavender and sage in the herb garden. And when Mama Inez brushes out her just-washed hair, leaning out of one of the tower windows, she watches the water droplets rush to the ground, and watches for bird shadows at the same time.

Mae's kestrel is the first to return, with its message of no.

"Not an auspicious beginning," Mama Inez tells Roberto and Franz two mornings later. She and Toby have negotiated the tricky tower steps with a feeling of nervousness. If the first reply is a no, what comes next?

But "Always worrying," is what Franz says.

"Let it rest. Wait and see."

"No use crying," Roberto chimes in, "until you know what you're crying about." His grin is wicked and funny at the same time. "I've heard that often enough."

Toby drinks milk and rubs his chocolate head against Mama Inez's leg. She sips her tea. "I suppose you're right," she says, the worry still there in her eyes.

But the next morning Mama Inez and Toby practically dance down the sixty-seven tower steps. She clutches a handful of thick rainbow-colored notes.

"Yes," she sings out, jubilant, as she comes into the kitchen. Franz and Roberto, arguing calmly about whether the plain gold band they're passing back and forth should have eyes, glance at her. There is no surprise on either face as she says, "Eight yeses!"

"Well, of course," Roberto says in a quiet way, and he goes back to his discussion.

❧❧

In the west, one person struggles to find the words, struggles to write them down. He still has trouble dealing with this world. Finally he simply writes, very carefully, "Yes," and sends the falcon on its way.

❧❧

Mama Inez is kneading bread when the last bird flutters outside the window. Toby sees it and gallops outside to retrieve it. He drops it at her feet. Mama Inez dusts the flour off her hands, unfolds the letter, and sees the careful printing. She breathes out a long breath and says, "Nine, then. A good number." And Toby barks and nods his big head.

❧❧

No matter what the state of the world, the market, with its buying and selling, laughing and haggling, dancing and sharing, is always a special event. Baskets and birdcages, weavings and whistles, fabrics and fruits—all change hands as people come to listen and to tell.

As the day wears on, as the moon is just starting to show her face, the market makes its first shift. The selling and buying are through, and now it's time for the dancing. Fiddle music begins to glide through the air, and it pulses like a heartbeat. Everyone, even Toby, begins the intricate weaving and passing, the hand clasping and clapping, the loud and soft footfalls that have been passed down from a time long forgotten.

Just before the dancing is through, Toby and Mama Inez disappear. Roberto and Franz never look in their direction as they glide into the gentle darkness that tugs on the edges of the dancing circle. They don't stop moving their feet, they don't raise an eyebrow. They know just where those two are going. They're on their way to the Indwelling and, from there, to the storytellers' tent. Franz and Roberto will join them there, and the market will shift once again.

Because Roberto has the gatherer instincts, he's been to the Indwelling several times. He's tried to tell Franz everything he's seen, but there's never been a way to describe the feeling of the place, the inner peace mixed with the thrumming excitement of stories that reflect the business of living.

Inside the Indwelling, it's just cool enough to be comfortable. The air smells of dust and salt and stars, and the moon reflects itself in the stream that divides the place into neat halves. There are shelves of varying widths that travel from the entrance, over the stream, and back to the opening that leads out into the night. The shelves are filled with squat raku and sunbaked jars the colors of the clay in the potter's room in the house with the witch's-hat roof. They're the exact right size to hold small treasures, and they have conical tops that make them look like beehives.

Toby walks across the stream, just outside the entrance, on a walkway of smooth stones. He walks back and forth seven times, and he makes sure that his paws are always dry. Then, his part of the beginning ritual complete, he sits and watches the moon's reflection rest on the water.

Mama Inez takes the purple jar she made just days ago. She raises it above her head, where the moon waits, leans down and holds it for several seconds against the reflected water moon, then stands slowly, sure to keep the jar level. Now, her half of the rite finished, she smiles at Toby, and the two of them leave to begin their night's work.

Even before she is back from the Indwelling, people gather beneath Mama Inez's tassel-draped, desert-gold canopy, waiting for stories. Some slouch on pillows big enough for three and drink the steam-coated spiced tea served in salt-glazed ceramic cups. Others sit at low, square tables, sip cold melon drinks, and rattle tiny ice cubes against the sides of thin glasses wrapped in silver filigree.

Mama Inez sees the waiting listeners, then sees her storytellers, a small moving amoeba of a group in the tellers' waiting area. Roberto is with them, looking something like a shepherd with a herd of wayward sheep. As Mama Inez and Toby come closer, they begin to hear snatches of conversation, to see the tellers' interactions.

Zola holds a length of midnight-blue cloth shot with gold. He's talking to a tall woman with a death grip on a basket of seashells: ". . . at the booth by the basket weaver's. It'll be a fine shirt for him. Make him look quite royal."

When the woman doesn't respond, Zola fidgets a bit, then adds, "Wouldn't you agree?"

The woman, who has no idea who Zola is talking about, nods, serious and nervous at the same time.

A large white horse, who looks as relaxed as he would if he were in his own stable, munches on a clump of grass. Periodically he pokes his head through an opening in the tent, as though keeping watch on someone. Every time he does this, a woman runs her fingers through his mane or holds her hand in front of his nose to feel his breath on her fingertips. She says very softly, "Lightning, I don't think we're at all in the right place. I mean, I guess this here's the end of the world, but I'm thinking that we don't fit in, not one bit. Everybody else looks right fancy. And like they know just what they're going to be doing."

Lightning glances at her, calm and easy. When a man with greenish-blond hair comes over and rubs Lightning's neck, then says, "He is a beautiful horse, madam," Lightning sniffs the stranger's hand, nods his head, and looks at Sue as if to say, "See? We're exactly where we should be," which makes Sue laugh.

Closer to the entryway than anyone stands Maddie, who clutches her twin. Even for an elf, she's quite pale. "Earl, I'll faint. Or you'll talk and distract me, and I'll lose track. Which will make me sound ridiculous, as if I have no brain."

"And that would be unusual because . . . ?"

"Earl," she moans.

"You were so thrilled when the invitation came," Earl says.

Maddie nods. "Before I saw all these people. Before I really knew what I'd have to do." She breathes out, hard, then looks at him and says, "You could do it, you know. I'd sit beside you and look quite interested."

"Oh, no. You were the one who most wanted to come, after all."

"Ummmm." Maddie breathes again. "At least promise you won't interrupt."

He flashes her an evil grin. "Only if you lose your place. Or faint."

Toby goes to stand by the most relaxed-looking person in the cluster. He doesn't look travel worn, like the man talking to Lightning. He's not nervous, like Maddie, and he seems completely comfortable, unlike Sue. He's smoking, in an absentminded kind of way, but when Toby comes near, he drops his cigarette and grinds it out in the dirt, then picks it up and puts it in his pocket. "No littering," he explains, and Toby taps his head against the man's knee.

Mama Inez follows Toby into the group. "I need," she begins—and the voices quiet immediately—"to thank you all. Tonight, with your help, we'll set the world in balance."

Rosey is wrapped in a shawl as red as Mama Inez's scarf. When Mama Inez first came back from the Indwelling, she pulled Rosey aside and hugged her, hard. Rosey hugged her grandmother back, her grandmother who lived at the end of the world and sometimes in Powton, near Rosey.

"When I sent your bird, I was worried that you might think that what happened wasn't important enough for a gathering," Mama Inez said then.

"I did," Rosey admitted. "But Samson said I was wrong."

"Excellent bird." Mama Inez held out her hand, and Samson snuggled in as if he belonged there.

Now Rosey stands next to a young woman who holds a smooth stone that periodically flashes in the moonlight. They look at each other. "I didn't think, even with all Gram's taught me about magic, that telling a story would be so intense," Rosey says. "I've been to gatherings before, but I've never been a teller."

"Hmm and well," says the other, "you've got me beat. I've never even been to one." Behind her, at the same time, Nodia's voice says, "B.J., I told you this was serious."

"Quiet, Nodia," says Wink, the second young man in their group of three. "Listen."

"If you could each give your talismans to Roberto, then he, Toby, and I will sequence them and give you the order of the tellings," says

Mama Inez. She looks at her crowd of calm, nervous, and uncertain people, and she adds, "Any questions?"

Wink raises his hand. "I've heard of this, you know. This market. This balancing." He pauses, then asks, "The need to do this—does it happen a lot?"

Mama Inez laughs her rich laugh. "Not a lot. But enough. And sometimes more than enough."

The woman with the flashing stone says, in a tight little voice, "But we're just . . . people. What if we're not strong enough to fix things?" The shifting of feet and the low murmurs around her show that this is what many are thinking.

Toby barks. Mama Inez says, "I agree with Toby. A group like this? I believe that you can conquer anything. And you must believe it, too, or you wouldn't be here."

"There's got to be some kind of truth right there. Something that hasn't happened to me, but something that I can learn from," Zola says to the woman with the shells, and he points to her basket.

The man with the greenish hair says, to Lightning and to Sue, "I do not know about me, but the two of you—you must have a story," and Sue looks at Lightning, thinks of Bill, and says, "You just might be right about that."

Mama Inez watches. She sees the man with the cigarette pat Toby, sees Earl steady Maddie, sees her group begin to grow in strength. She smiles and says, "Has everyone given their talisman to Roberto?"

Roberto, Toby, and Mama Inez huddle in the north corner of the tellers' waiting area, shifting the talismans on a table covered with a cloth the color of spring grass. The purple jar from the

Indwelling sits at the top left corner, anchoring the cloth, an iris of color. On the far left: a green brocade ribbon from the man with the greenish hair. Next to it is a whorled shell from the woman with the basket, and a thick gold coin from the man who won't litter. Then a tiny leather slipper, from the twins. The river stone that flashes in the moonlight. A small glass star from the group of three, and a golden pea from the man with the midnight-blue cloth. A piece of white lace comes from Sue and Lightning. And finally, red wool from Rosey.

Mama Inez runs her fingers along the bottom of the talismans. She looks at Toby and Roberto. "Agreed?" Toby puts his head on the table, then barks. Roberto thinks of the rings he and Franz have made, then nods. Mama Inez turns back to the waiting crowd and makes her announcements.

The Lizard Man, hearing that he's to be first, bows his head. His greenish hair drapes around his face, and his breathing is shallow. Sue notices. She and Lightning smile at him, and Sue gives him a small push toward Mama Inez and the entrance to the part of the tent that holds the teller's cushion. "Ya'll be fine," she says. "Done before you know it." He smiles a bleak smile and moves with slow, measured steps through the tent opening.

Mama Inez watches him, remembering her time in the Lizard's story. And the Lizard Man? He feels a remembering, too, one of color. Mama Inez's hair is the same color as a mouse he once knew.

The Lizard's Tale

"I NEVER WANTED TO be anything but a lizard. That rat, that stupid rat Malvolio who became the coach driver—he'd always had dreams of being something bigger, something better than he was. But me, I was content living in the garden between the cistern and the downspout, soaking up sun and wind, water and air."

Mama Inez sees him stumble and nods encouragement; watches him take a breath, shift his gaze to the rear of the tent, and begin again.

"I never wanted to be anything but a lizard.

"Then that fairy godmother comes along with her magic wand, her high-flying notions. And as fast as a snap from two fingers I am six feet tall, dressed in green brocade, strands of greenish blond hair dipping into my eye and clubbed into a knot at the base of my neck. My brain feels huge, stuffed into my head. And it is filled with thoughts that I have no names for.

"That rat Malvolio is prancing around the court-yard like a rearing stallion. He has new long legs, like me. He shakes his head, and his silver rat whiskers, which are now short and covering the lower half of his face, sparkle in the moonlight.

"'Look at me,' he is chittering. 'Watch me! See this wonderful thing I've become.'

"He spins on his feet and immediately falls to the ground in a clatter of buttons and boots. He skids on the courtyard cobbles and ends up lying half under a pumpkin stripped of its innards and forced into the shape of a carriage. The pumpkin is harnessed to three timid-looking white horses and one bold black one. All are covered with hair that looks soft as mouse fur.

"'Stop that,' says that godmother. She is the one who turned the pumpkin into a coach with a second wave of her wand. She pulls Malvolio upright. 'You must listen to me. The cinder girl will be here any moment. You must be presentable, in control, or she'll be afraid to ride with you. She's a nervous little thing. Always has been.'

"That godmother is brushing at the back of Malvolio's pants now, trying to slap away the dust. I watch them, leaning heavily against the wall of the barn. I feel shaky and suddenly sick. If Cindergirl, whoever she is, will not like a dancing rat, what will she think of a vomiting lizard?

"Then a soft voice says, 'Godmother?' and I turn in the direction of the sound. Standing before me is the most beautiful sight I have ever seen. My first thought is that this must be Cindergirl. My other thoughts jumble and mix. There is a swelling in my chest, a rapid beating in my heart, a buzzing in my head. I feel woozy. I feel air on my tongue and know that my mouth must be open.

"'Godmother? Is this . . . right? Do I look like someone who could go the ball? Or will they all laugh at me?' She fidgets. Her fingers brush her dress, hesitating between strokes. She catches her lower lip between small, white, perfect teeth.

"I know the Queen of the Lizards is the most striking, most peerless of us all, though I have never seen her. But Cindergirl must be more beautiful than the queen herself. Her gown shimmers as if the stars have fallen and been captured in its folds. Her hair, a shining gold, hangs in long curls, captured on one side in a ribbon of green. Her feet, those feet that would have been near my nose minutes before, are covered with clear, shining glass slippers.

"I choke back a tiny noise, and in spite of the uncomfortable feelings in my gut, in my head, I push myself off the wall and stand as tall as I am able. I will look proper for Cindergirl. I will look like a man.

"'Godmother?' She shivers slightly in the autumn air, hunches her shoulders.

"'You look exactly like someone who should go to the ball,' that godmother promises. 'The prince will be enchanted.'

"This makes Cindergirl smile, and that smile makes me catch and hold my breath.

"'Just remember,' that godmother says, 'to be home by midnight. Otherwise you'll be helping a rat and some lizards drag home a pumpkin.'

"She smiles again. 'I'll remember.' They embrace, and I hear Cindergirl whisper, 'Oh, Godmother, thank you,' and that fairy saying, 'Don't forget. Twelve o'clock.'

"Then, with a rustle of fabric and beads that delights my ears, She begins to climb into the pumpkin coach. I hurry to assist her, almost falling over my own foreign feet. I manage to catch Cindergirl's elbow, and the feel of that skin against mine is like the touch of the silkiest flower that ever bloomed.

"That rat Malvolio has already made his way to the coachman's box and is wiggling the reins of the mouse horses. I, having no confidence in him, think he is trying to figure out how to drive. If he makes a mistake, if Cindergirl is hurt, I will kill him. I hiss this at him as I pass, and he looks down at me, surprised.

"I clamber on the back of the coach, as close to her as I can get."

He pauses.

"I have no pictures in my mind of what happens inside during the ball. I wait outside with Malvolio and the mice. There are other lizards with us, lizards who are footmen, like me. They taste the air by flicking their tongues. They push their fine sleeves up to their elbows to feel the cool breezes on their skin. I do none of these things. Instead, I watch for Cindergirl, standing tall and still. Not like a lizard, like a man.

"We can hear music, and again Malvolio tries to dance. Even I can see that he is terrible at this, but he insists. His dream of being something new and different has come true, and now he must try everything he has ever wanted, everything he has ever hoped for.

"I listen closely whenever the bells in the tower above my head bong. I now know the little tune that comes halfway between each series of bongs, and I know that this means it is halfway between the longer bongs of the hours. I understand how to count, something I never understood before. I think this must be another gift from that godmother, given to me to help Cindergirl get home by the right time. I count carefully, as if my life depends upon it. Last time there were eleven bongs. Eleven hours. That godmother said twelve o'clock. She must be home before twelve. By progression, twelve is the next number. I watch the wide stone palace steps, watch for Cindergirl to appear.

"Then Cindergirl is there, half running toward us. Toward me. She is laughing, looking over her shoulder. I run to meet her, afraid that she might trip, stumble in her shiny glass slippers. I touch her elbow, guiding her to the coach. A man in fancy, soft clothing follows us closely, begging her to stay. The prince that god-mother spoke of?

"'No, no. I must leave, Your Highness. Perhaps I'll see you tomorrow. There's still a night of dancing tomorrow, is there not?' She flicks her golden curls over her shoulder and smiles. She does not seem ner-vous now.

"'Yes,' he calls as I tuck Cindergirl into the coach. 'Yes. Tomorrow.' His voice is desperate.

"She settles in the coach with a happy sigh, almost closing my fingers in the door.

"We make it back to our courtyard just as the

distant palace clock begins to count twelve in the moist night air. I hurry to open her door, to remove Cindergirl from the coach before it once again becomes a pumpkin. Before I once again become a lizard. But she ignores my hand, stepping out on her own, and as she does, a barely audible pop sounds in the air. The coach shrinks back to a largish pumpkin, the footmen are once again lizards, the horses turn back to mice. Cindergirl's clothes are no longer fine things one would wear to a palace, but are instead plain, homespun wool. She is even more beautiful this way. The only thing left is the green hair ribbon, twisted in the dirt. The black mouse watches as I pick it up and put it in my vest pocket.

"But that is not a lizard thing to do, and as I realize this, I see that my eyes are still very far from the ground. I am still dressed in green brocade. Malvolio is still in his coachman's suit. That godmother, I think helplessly as the other lizards scuttle away, has got it all wrong. Or—and this thought makes me feel as ill as when I was transformed—maybe it is Malvolio and I who are wrong.

"I watch dumbly as Cindergirl goes into the house, singing. She does not seem to notice us. The black mouse sits by my boot, her eyes moving between the door and me."

"We do it all again the next night.

"When that fairy godmother shows up, I try to talk to her. She looks at me in surprise, because I am changed even though she has not yet cast her spell. Then she takes two steps back, and her eyes show fear.

"But now Cindergirl is here, ready for another night with the prince. My heart beats as rapidly as before when I see her. For her, I will do anything. I will even remain a man. I think that perhaps it is something like this, something like love or desire, that has made

Malvolio and me retain our man shapes. I am no longer a lizard. He is no longer a rat. We both have exactly what we want. Perhaps life is all in the wishing.

"That godmother turns away from me, looking relieved to see Cindergirl, and waves her wand. Tonight, that wand shakes."

"At half past eleven I wait quietly, halfway up the wide palace steps, but Cindergirl does not come out. I climb higher, beginning to worry. The tower clock plays off the next tune, the one that comes closer to the hour bongs. She is not here.

"I climb higher still. I am almost at the palace door. The guard there is staring at me.

"The tower clock begins to strike again, and suddenly there she is. She sees me, recognizes me, runs straight toward me. I feel a flutter of pure happiness deep in my chest.

"Now we are running hard down those stone steps.

The bonging of the tower clock, the clicking of her slippers, the thudding of my boots—all echo through the night. On the last step Cindergirl slips, almost tumbles, but my strong arm is there to help her. We make it to the carriage, which is already beginning to stink of old pumpkin, and Malvolio lashes the mouse horses into a frenzy. As we roll away, I see the prince at the top of the stairs, the glitter of a glass slipper at the bottom.

"We are barely past the palace gates when I hear the pop again and that godmother's transformation undoes itself. Coach returns to pumpkin, horses to mice, footmen to lizards. Everything is what is meant to be. Everything except for me and Malvolio. The black mouse follows me, running hard. I pick her up and put her in my pocket, and she wiggles her whiskers against my palm. We leave the other mice to take care of themselves. We kick the pumpkin into the weeds to rot on the side of the road. We escort Cindergirl home, but she does not seem to notice that we are behind her.

"The next day, everywhere there are criers. 'Whoever has the foot to fit this slipper shall marry the prince.'

"Cindergirl's foot is dainty and perfect, just like she herself. No one else can wear that shoe. Still, there are lines of fine ladies pushing and shoving. Not acting fine at all. Curling their toes, trying to force their feet into the shoe. One of Cindergirl's stepsisters shows up in the back garden with a butcher knife. I wonder if the sister will cut off her own toes if need be.

"Cindergirl stays inside. Her stepsisters have forced her to clean the cellar. She cleans, and cries. She has been crying since early this morning. I saw her then, and I see her now when I peer through the window on the garden side of the house, the side near my cistern. I think Cindergirl did not want to leave her prince. I think she may not have heard the crier. I think she does not know the prince is looking for her.

"Should I tell? I wonder. If I do not, I will keep

Cindergirl for my own. We will move to a good place, a better place than this, and I will make her happy. No more cleaning cellars. No more crying.

"The stepsisters rush down the stairs to the cellar, one limping, her foot wrapped in a reddened towel. She leaves bloody blotches behind her. 'It didn't work,' she is screaming. 'It was supposed to work!'

"'Fix her,' the other sister yells, shoving the girl toward Cindergirl. 'Fix her foot before she bleeds to death.'

"She looks at them, eyes huge and shiny with tears. I can hear the prince and the crier getting ready to leave. Then the black mouse is next to me. She stands on her hind legs, and her tiny paws tug at my pants. My stomach feels full of rocks, my heart emptied of blood, but I know the mouse is right. I must get Cindergirl to the prince. I pound on the window. I will do anything for her.

"'Hurry,' I cry. 'Hurry, before the prince leaves.'

"They all turn, all stare at me, but on Cindergirl's face I see a flash of recognition.

"'Hurry,' I cry again, and I see Cindergirl turn from her stepsisters. They do not move as quickly as they might otherwise have done. One, after all, now has only blood where her toes should be. The other seems torn between stopping Cindergirl and helping her sister. I see Cindergirl's foot touch the bottom cellar stair.

"I run to stop the prince from leaving. Cindergirl is close behind me, having come straight up those stairs and out the back door.

"'Wait, Highness,' I cry. 'There is one more lady who has not yet tried the shoe.'

"The prince stops and sees Cindergirl, who runs to meet him. Happiness lights his face.

"The slipper, of course, fits perfectly.

"Now my crying is in my eyes, not in my voice. I watch Cindergirl ride away with her prince. Malvolio follows, his questions of how he may serve the court lingering in the air. I do not see Cindergirl look back, although I watch, through wet eyes, for a very long time.

"Cindergirl has been gone for many days. I count each day as carefully as I counted the sounds of the hours from the palace clock on those nights when I was dressed in brocade. Now I wear rough homespun that I have stolen from a neighbor's stableboy. I try to do jobs I am not suited for. Kitchen work, fetching and carrying. Jobs that make me feel clumsy. And stupid. The only goodness I feel is in the black mouse, who has been my constant companion.

"Life may be in the wishing, but try as I may, I have not been able to wish myself back to my lizard shape. I search for that godmother every day, whenever I am not being called upon to do some chore. She seems to have disappeared.

"And then, there she is, that fairy godmother, walk-ing through the garden with another lady, collecting herbs in a little grass basket. I drop the bucket I am supposed to be filling and hear it crack as it hits the cobbles. Water leaks through the broken staves. I do not stop to try to fix my mistake, even though I can hear the cook screaming at me from inside the kitchen.

"'You!' I cry, running at her, fast as I would have run away from the cat in my lizard shape. 'You! Make me whole again.'

"That godmother turns at the sound of my voice, turns to see who calls out to her. She recognizes me, I can tell, because her face, pink from the sun that brightens this day, pink from the stooping to gather lavender and sage and parsley, turns the color of new milk. I am close enough to her to hear her friend, the other lady, say, 'Who is that?'

"That godmother tosses her head and answers, 'I have no idea.' But I know that she is lying.

"Even with only two legs, I cover the ground quickly, because these legs are long. I grab that godmother by the arm, making her, by accident, drop her little gathering basket. 'Please,' I beg. 'I do not want to stay in this shape. Let me go back to what I was. Let me forget about these man feelings.'

"Her friend is holding her other arm, as if she is afraid I will take that godmother away. But I only want to return to my lizard self. 'Please,' I repeat.

"That godmother shakes her head at me. 'Go away, young man. I can do nothing for you.'

"'You have not even tried,' I say, but she shakes my fingers from her arm, grabs her basket, and quickly walks away. Her friend looks back at me over her shoulder. She looks at me like I am a bad person. Just before they turn the corner near the cistern, that godmother meets my eyes. She shrugs her shoulders and shakes her head. Then she and her friend disappear.

"'Leave! Go away!' The cook has come into the garden and is screaming. 'All you ever do is make messes. Leave here at once.' And her finger is pointing at me.

"That godmother cannot help me. Or will not. Either way, I am stuck in this shape. What will I do? I think hard, trying not to listen to the cook. I turn toward the palace, but I feel a tug on my pant leg that makes me look down. The black mouse is watching me, and her head shakes no. I keep my eyes on her as I turn a slow circle in the yard. Only when my back is to the palace does she nod, seeming satisfied.

"So I decide to do as the mouse says. I will go, as Malvolio did, but I will go in a different way. I turn my back on that screaming cook, on my garden, on the cistern and the downspout, and I walk away from the direction that Cindergirl and her prince went those many days ago. The little black mouse watches me leave.

"I will find something to do in some other place. There must be one thing I can be good at. And soon, soon, I will forget Cindergirl. When that happens, fairy godmother or not, I will return to myself. Then, lizard or man, I will be at peace."

People clap, and the Lizard Man, straight and proud, walks away from the teller's cushion. Watching him, Mama Inez is well pleased. She remembers how long she stayed with him in her mouse form, how long she watched him, how she tried to help him see what he could do with his new, human life. Seeing him, hearing his confidence grow as he told his story, she feels assured that he's picked a good path for himself.

Now she looks for her next teller. Renata still clutches her basket of shells. She's given the pink one, the one that most reminds her of Clarisse, to Mama Inez. Still, having the rest makes Clarisse feel closer, makes Renata feel that she has a second voice to help her tell this story. She's more nervous than she's ever been, but she remembers the man with the cloth, the one who was so excited about making that shirt. He said he felt he could learn from her. And if that was the case, maybe someone else could learn something, too. As she watched the Lizard Man, she listened carefully and tried to learn from the things he did.

Now she looks at the moon and sees its reflection in the mirrors on Mama Inez's scarf. She thinks of her own moon and of waves lapping on the sands. She walks through the tent flap, eyes straight ahead, shoulders back.

Mama Inez stands to one side as Renata goes to the teller's cushion. She, too, looks at the moon, feels its strength, and remembers her own moon bond on those two nights not all that long ago.

Renata sits on the golden cushion. Her basket of shells is next to her right foot. One hand rests on the large brown-and-white shell that's shifted to take the place of her pink talisman shell. She draws a long breath that pulls her into her story.

Conversions

"SOME OF YOU MAY remember the tales of the Merfolk, but in case you don't, let me tell you. They're water people, but they have the ability to stay on land if one of two things happens: they fall in love with a human and want to stay, or they're captured by a human and forced to stay. Either way, fins turn into legs." She pauses, then adds, "From what I've heard, it can be quite painful."

The audience mutters.

"True. Even when one is in love, pain, actual physical pain, may make things so difficult that one needs to return to the sea, no matter how much it costs. For those forced to stay, life can be unbearable."

More mutterings, some angry.

"Sometimes the legend works in reverse. And it comes without the pain, or so I hope."

❦

"I still remember the smell of the sea, the grit of the sand, the color of Vachel's blood. Especially the color of that blood.

"My first reaction was to turn away from the shadowy shape on the beach.

"'We can't just leave him there,' Clarisse told me. She grabbed my shoulders and twisted me around. 'He's dying. Look at him, Renata. Really look!'

"I really looked, and damn it, she was right. Later I wished I hadn't looked. Then everything would have been different. I bit my lip, trying not to breathe too deeply, and approached the Mer. Clarisse was tight against me. 'Do you think he'll understand us?' I asked softly.

"'I don't know. Do you know his language? Because I don't.'

"I could write the word 'door' in hieroglyphics. I'd taken some Welsh in school and knew the words for 'father' and 'mother.' I could also say 'banana' and 'gorilla' in the tongue of my forefathers. Right now none of this seemed at all useful. 'No,' I sighed. 'Of course not.'

"'Then we'll try normal, everyday speech,' Clarisse said.

"Now that I was helping, she was ready to take charge, so I shoved her in front of me. She stopped just short of touching distance and said, in a clear, slow voice, 'Are you hurt?'

"'Stupid question. You just said he was dying,' I hissed.

"The Mer didn't answer, but his eyes flicked toward us. They were the blue of the sea that rippled behind him. It was just far enough away that it couldn't take him back to his world and had left him in our place instead: a place where you need legs, not fins.

"'We want to help.' Clarisse moved fractionally closer and reached down to touch his shoulder.

"He yanked his body out of her reach, moving frantically. 'No!' The one syllable seemed torn from him. It was accented with an inflection I'd never heard before. But right then, that didn't seem important. When he'd shifted, I'd seen the long blue gash on his chest. The edges were flayed and wet, and the wound looked deep.

"'Do Mer have blood?' I asked.

"Clarisse looked up at me. 'How should I know?' she almost yelled. 'I'm sure there's something inside to make them work.'

"'Well, if they've got blood, that might be what's leaking from that cut on his chest.'

"'Ah. I get it,' she said, and she didn't even come close to yelling this time. In fact, she now seemed interested, in a strange, tender kind of way. She tried to touch him again and he tried to pull away, but it was obvious that he'd used up most of his strength with his last move.

"I inched over to his other side. 'Let's both try to turn him over. He seems to be able to understand some of what we say. He answered us, after all. He ought to be able to tell that we aren't going to hurt him.'

"'The word 'no' hardly qualifies as answering. And would you trust us if you were him?'

"I thought about the ones who caught them. They'd bodysurf on the Mers' backs, foot to fin, chest to back, fingers digging hard into the muscled shoulders, faces brushing the braided hair. Something I thought of as a nasty master-slave relationship, but that Mer riders described as 'incredible fun.' They'd use them after they cut them from the nets, wear them out, then abandon them. If they went back to the sea, fine. They could always catch more. If they didn't, fine, too. It hardly seemed to matter. Sometimes I'd find the dead bodies on the shore, empty shells, the iridescent gleam long gone from their bronze-colored skins.

"But finding dead bodies was better than finding live ones, like this. Bodysurfing was one thing. Actually talking to a Mer, that was something else. Mers were untouchables unless they were being used. There were laws about dealing with untouchables.

"I didn't go to the beach much.

"I shook my head in answer to Clarisse's question. Of course I wouldn't trust us. 'But I still think we need to see that wound on his chest,' I said.

"We approached from opposite directions, moving carefully even though he seemed way too exhausted to fight.

"Clarisse's voice sounded like warm honey. 'We only want to help. We can get you back to the water if you're okay.'

"I stopped halfway down to his shoulder. 'How?' I asked her, shocked. He was big, both long and strongly developed. I doubted that both of us could drag him the two feet it would take to make it to the shallows, and even if we could, that still wouldn't be deep enough.

"She glared at me, so I stopped talking and leaned closer to his right side. That was when I realized that I'd been breathing normally for some time now. I stopped moving again. 'He doesn't smell. Smell bad, I mean.' I sounded surprised, even to myself.

"Clarisse shook her head. 'Just like the sea. I've always wondered if they knew what they were talking about.'

"'Fear,' he said.

"We both jumped back.

"'We smell of fear. When they catch us.' His speech was careful, the accent making him hard to understand. 'When they—ride us.' This last sentence was spoken so softly, I almost missed it. He sounded ashamed.

"'Of course,' Clarisse said. She sounded practical and calm. 'I would, too.'

"He turned his head and looked up at her, straining

his neck. From where I stood, I could see the tendons stretch. She crouched near his shoulder.

"'Can we turn you? To look at your wound?'

"His nod was slow in coming, but at least he seemed willing to let us touch him now. We rolled him between us, slowly, carefully. The cut looked like something intentional, something made with a fishing knife. Under the bronze skin, the layers of flesh were blue tinged, the gore around the wound almost the same color as his eyes. Clarisse winced visibly, face paling, then raised her eyes to mine over his body.

"'You've got to know more than I do about this kind of stuff.'

"'Why?'

"'Because I don't know anything. Should it be stitched, or can we just bandage it?'

"I shook my head. Then I put very gentle pressure on the skin on either side of the cut. He didn't say anything, didn't even moan, but his eyes snapped shut and sweat broke out on his upper lip. I yanked my hands back nervously and said, 'If we want him to be able to get home, I think it'll need stitches. The pull of the water alone would just wreck any kind of bandage that I can think of.'

"'And if he decides to stay here?'

"Her question was casual enough, but she wouldn't look at me fully. I sat in the sand with my mouth open for a bit too long. I finally said, 'Clarisse, how could he stay here? Why would he stay here?'

"'I do not think that would be possible,' he said over my questions. 'We die if we stay here. We need the sea.' His eyes were looking directly at Clarisse. He wasn't even making an attempt to make it look like I was included. I could hardly believe what was happening right there in front of me. Clarisse, the one who hadn't even looked at the opposite sex since a nasty breakup over two years ago, was now sitting right here, on the beach, locking eyes with an alien species.

"'Hey.' I tried to break the invisible string that was holding their eyes together. It didn't really work. I sighed. 'It still needs stitches. This is deep and it's still . . . bleeding.' I watched the blue liquid seeping down his chest, wondering if I'd used the right word.

"'Yes,' he whispered, as if I'd asked him directly.

"I nodded. 'Stitches,' I repeated firmly.

"The string finally broke. Clarisse looked at me and said, 'Where? There's not a hospital anywhere that'd take him. You know that. Not any doctor I can think of, either, who'd be willing to take that kind of a risk.'

"'No Mer pay-as-you-go plans?' I said, trying to lighten things up. Clarisse looked like she wanted to smack me.

"'Look,' I said hurriedly. 'We might be able to fix it ourselves. Your place is closer. If we could get him there . . .'

"She was already on her feet. 'I'll get the Beast. You wait.'

"She'd turned away, running, before I could answer her. After the sound of her feet slapping the sand had died away, I tried not to think about what would happen if I were found alone at dusk with a Mer anywhere close to life. The words 'criminal offense' kept running through my mind. We looked at each other for what seemed like a long time. His skin was drying, turning dull. His eyes seemed less blue than they had before, but that may only have been because it was getting darker. Finally, to hear the sound of something other than the incessant pull of the sea, I said, 'What's your name?'

"My speech seemed to give him more trouble than Clarisse's. I could almost see him puzzling out the words. Finally he said, 'Vachel. I am called Vachel. And you?'

"'Renata.' He was very polite to even pretend

to care. 'She's Clarisse,' I added, pointing to where Clarisse had disappeared.

"He nodded, then asked quietly, 'I will make trouble for you?'

"Watching him steadily, I said, 'Only if we get caught. And only if you're still alive when we do.'

"He nodded again, as though I'd confirmed everything he'd ever heard about us, and I realized at that moment that his sources were more accurate than mine. I'd never really believed that the Mer had only the basest intelligence, that they didn't object to the 'fun' of being ridden, that they tangled themselves in the nets on purpose to meet their 'gods.' I'd never really believed it, but when you've heard the tales since you were a kid, sometimes it's hard not to believe.

"'Vachel,' I said loudly, using his name to make him hear, to make sure he was still awake and aware. Dusk was giving way to true night, but even taking the darkness into account, his eyes looked too cloudy, and his breathing was off-kilter in a way that scared me. Where the hell was Clarisse? I had to keep him alert, conscious. 'How do you know our language? Is that your . . . people's language, too?' Was 'people' right?

"He flicked his eyelids as if trying to clear his vision. His voice was soft, and I had to lean closer to hear. 'Many years ago, one of your kind fell in love with a Mer. He was willing to give up his life on land to be with her. There is a way this can be done, though it can never be undone. He lived with her under the sea. The language he brought with him was handed down through generations. It mingled with our own, which is more sounds than words, and became a kind of second language for us.'

"'That sounds like a fairy tale.'

"He shifted restlessly on the sand. 'A what?'

"I would have tried to explain, but the lights of Clarisse's vintage SUV flashed across the sand. The thing weighed a ton, had a perpetual air of neglect, smelled of something too long near the water that never quite dried out. It always seemed on the verge of stalling, and she had to pop the clutch every time she downshifted to keep it running. I was overjoyed to see it.

"Getting Vachel into the Beast was very nasty and extremely difficult. He helped as much as he could, but even with those shoulder muscles pushing him up, there was a large amount of dragging and yanking and pulling. I know we hurt him. By the time we were done, Clarisse and I were sweating in the cool night air, and covered with sand and salt. But Vachel lay curled in the back of the Beast. His fins were covered with an old blanket splattered with mildew stains and coated with bits of shell and seaweed, and he was panting, clearly exhausted. Clarisse, breath back under control, looked at him, scrambled into the front, said, 'Renata! Get in!' and headed back across the beach like the hounds of hell were behind her. The Beast lurched and rolled, but it kept moving, and right then, that was all I could ask.

"During the short trip to Clarisse's building, I told her what Vachel had said while she'd been gone. The expression in her eyes when she looked at me was unfocused and distant. She didn't say anything, just stopped with a sharp jerk in an illegal space near the door closest to the entrance.

"Now all we had to do was get him through the door, across the hall, up in the hand-operated elevator, and across another hall to her rooms. We looked at each other hopelessly. Vachel's breath sounded harsh in the seat behind us.

"Then Clarisse sat up straight. I could see her clearly in the iridescent moonlight. Through some trick of the atmosphere, the source of that light looked like it held the face of a woman with long, thick hair. Clarisse's eyes were bright, as if she were going to cry. 'I'm asking Michael. He could carry him.'

"I snatched at her wrist, horrified at the suggestion. 'You can't! I know he's always seemed like a decent guy, but you can't tell how he feels about them.'

"She started to speak, and I cut across her words. 'No one ever talks about that. Don't even try to tell me you did, because I won't believe you.'

"'Fine,' she said, her voice quavering. 'We never talked about Mer. But we have talked about other things. And I think he'll be okay.' The tears were running freely down her cheeks now. 'If I don't, he'll die. Renata . . .'

"I dropped my forehead down into my hands. 'I know. Damn it.'

"Michael lived next door to Clarisse. He was as tall as Vachel was long. He swam and surfed (although I never, not even once, suspected him of being a Mer rider) and had a body that matched—strong arms and a broad chest. Now that I thought about it, he had a Mer's body, without the fins.

"Clarisse was back in less time than I expected, Michael a looming dark shape behind her. The strange moonlight seemed to be trying to hide us, and everyone looked like shadows on shadows, etched with tarnished silver.

"Michael didn't say a word. He just nodded at me and opened the door of the Beast. In the low light I could see Vachel open his eyes. Even in the dimness, the panicky look on his face made me want to weep.

"Michael, after sizing up the situation, said only, 'Renata, get on the other side and slide him out while we pull.' He looked at the Mer. 'Vachel, right?' Vachel nodded warily. Michael said, 'Michael Townsend. It's going to hurt, I think.'

"'Yes,' Vachel whispered. His adrenaline, or whatever Mer have, must have been pumping like crazy. The sea smell of him was very strong.

"'Okay, Renata,' Michael said. 'Push him toward us.'

"My adrenaline was pumping, too. I wondered briefly what I smelled like to the Mer. Then I began the horrible job of pushing his gritty shoulders across the seat. Vachel screamed only once, low in his throat, and bit the sound back almost immediately.

"Michael and Clarisse were having a terrible time finding something solid to latch onto near his fins. Vachel's body twisted and almost slipped as he tried to help. This time I was the one who cried out. Finally Michael was holding the long body in his arms, breathing heavily. Clarisse was standing close to Vachel's head, speaking softly and, from what I could hear, saying nothing that made any sense at all.

"Michael's arms were shaking by the time we made it to Clarisse's door. He missed stepping on the lucky crab drawn on the hall floor, skidding his foot onto the doorsill instead. A sure sign of bad times to come. I saw him realize what he'd done and turn slightly pale, but he didn't try to go back, only kept walking, heading for the couch. Clarisse insisted he keep going, though—into the bathroom. She started running water over Vachel as soon as he was propped in her tiny tub. His eyes were screwed shut and the gash on his chest looked worse, but color started to come back into his skin once he was wet. When the tub was half full, Clarisse left, then came back with a round pink box of salt. She dumped the whole thing in the water. Vachel managed a weak smile.

"I was more thankful than I could possibly say when I found out that Michael had taken a first-aid class. He'd even once put emergency stitches in a friend's arm. 'Reginald,' he said as he threaded his needle, 'surfed right into the rocks that edge those thick waves at Strather's Beach.' I shuddered. I knew those rocks. They were by a sea so violent that no one ever dared try to surf a Mer there. Michael saw my reaction and grinned. 'Reginald always was an idiot.'

"Then he turned his attention to Vachel, and I boiled things and found peroxide. Once Michael had everything he needed, I didn't even pretend to watch. Instead, I sat on the broken-tiled floor of the bathroom, making pictures out of the cracks in the wall above the shower nozzle until Michael was finished.

"When I couldn't find any more pictures in the cracks, I watched Clarisse, on her knees, squeezing Vachel's hand. I was hurting more for her than for him, for reasons I didn't want to name. Vachel made it through two full stitches before he passed out. Even then, she didn't stop talking to him. I don't know what she said. She barely knew him, and yet I was sure that I was watching the most intimate thing I'd ever seen in my life.

"Once Michael had finished his medical treatment, we didn't know what to do with him, or for him. But Mer must have some astounding powers of recovery. Within two days Vachel was up and moving, or moving as much as a Mer can on land. I stayed at Clarisse's, willing to do anything I could to help. Whenever we needed a bathroom, we went over to Michael's. He finally just left his front door unlocked, day and night.

"We all took care of Vachel, but it was Clarisse Vachel wanted to see, no matter how polite he was to all of us. And vice versa.

"I told Michael the story of the man living under the sea one afternoon when the sun came through the dusty windows in golden bars and warmed the faded rug in Clarisse's living room. 'But it's got to be a fairy tale, right?' I looked toward the bathroom. 'She wouldn't go with him—she couldn't. Could she?'

"I wanted him to say no. Unequivocally no. Instead, he gazed past me and said, 'Water's a wonderful and amazing thing. It carries your mind and it carries your body. It can caress you and it can kill you. One's as easy as the other.'

"I glanced up, confused. He stood in the newly-churned-butter light in front of the couch, looking down at me. 'I guess what I'm saying is I don't know. Renata, I just—don't know.'

"I remembered Michael's foot missing the lucky crab. I think I'd been waiting for the bad times ever since we'd brought Vachel home. It looked like they were on the way. I watched Michael in that yellow light, and I started to cry.

"I guess fairy tales can come true after all. Vachel and Clarisse slipped into the sea when the moon was the egg shape it gets just before it turns full. The same face I'd seen the night we found Vachel was back. This time, the woman was smiling, and the light coming down was the color of new pearls.

"Gossamer webs of moonlight swept over the waves. Michael and I stood in the sand, and I swear, just before Clarisse disappeared, I saw her legs mold into a fin. But who knows? That strange moonlight might have played tricks on my eyes."

❧❧

"I've moved into Clarisse's rooms. They're so much nicer than mine. Michael comes over a lot. Noodles with hot green sauce; beer; and word games. Tomato flatbread, rice wine, and dice. We're building our own story, just like I imagine Clarisse and Vachel are doing. Ours is, of course, land-bound. But then, everyone's story is different.

"We spend a lot of our nights on the beach. I get excited every time bottles or fishing balls wash up onto the sand. I grab them and hold them up to the moon, looking for the note I expect to find inside. Someday I'll get a message from Clarisse."

❧❧

Renata unfolds herself from the cushion. Her audience is murmuring, this time in approval. She leaves the teller's area, feeling parched from talking for so long, and comes face-to-face with Roberto, who offers her a cup of lemon tea. Renata takes the tea and smiles.

Mama Inez smiles, too. She says, "Nicely told." Renata thanks her, her eyes held by the flashes of the moon mirrors on Mama Inez's scarf.

Renata knows that moon. She starts to speak, but before she can, Mama Inez says, "You live near a beautiful sea."

Renata says, "I thought you might have seen it." She gives Mama Inez one more shell, a gold one flecked with blue. "Now you can hear it, too," she says.

Pleased with the mood of the night, her shell cupped in her hand, Mama Inez turns around, and John is right there.

"I am the next victim, right?" he asks. There's a snap in his eyes, enough to let her know this is a joke.

"You are," she answers, a laugh rumbling in her voice.

John reaches into his pocket, takes out a gold

coin that matches his talisman, spins it with a practiced hand, and then, with a twist of his wrist, twirls it. The coin flips through the air, flashing colors of pink and yellow. Mama Inez sets her shell on the ground and holds out her hand. As if it's a homing pigeon, the coin lands in the exact center of her palm. Like returning to like.

"I thought I recognized you," John says, and he walks out to his waiting audience. Mama Inez nods. She remembers just how it felt to be a coin tossed from the cloud shape Toby had become. She can feel the flat spin, can see the sun flashing red and gold, and can remember exactly how it felt to land smack in the center of John's palm, with the warmth of his hand curled around wavy edges. "Magic on top of magic," she says.

Once in front of the crowd, John tries to adjust his thinking. Giving something away is hard for him. It goes against his merchant sensibility. Giving something personal away is even harder. He looks at the waiting crowd. They appear to be ready for a good story. He sees Franz and Roberto sitting together, discussing their rings sotto voce. They glance his way, then set aside a tapered piece made of silver and gold. Mama Inez stands by the entrance to the teller's area, John's coin flashing in her hand. Toby sits on his haunches, expectant. Everything John sees lets him know just how much they want what he has to give. He breathes three times, nods to Toby as he would to a prince, and begins to spin his story into the web of the evening.

Beanstalks in Enlay

"WHEN JACK, THE LAZIEST fellow around, first tried to sell me the beans and told me to plant them, my assumption was that he was trying to get out of work. Again. You see, I knew Jack, and I knew that even the little amount of work it would take to dig three small holes, drop in the three warm, shiny beans, cover them up, and give them a little water now and again was three times as much work as that boy was likely to do. Getting a few coins for them would be so much simpler.

"And when he whispered 'Magic beans' to me, I laughed right in his face. 'Magic beans' my ass. Of course, I was more cynical then than I am now.

"I've always been a traveling merchant. I followed in my father's footsteps. But I differed from him, too. My father could never stay in one place for longer than one or two days. When I was only a boy, my mother despaired of ever taming him and took me, and herself, to Enlay to set up what she called 'a real life.'

"I tried to take the best of both of them. I traveled, but I always came home. Which is why I knew all about Jack.

"'You could sell these beans yourself, John, after they grow,' he said to me, but he must have seen the doubt in my eyes, because he kept talking. 'You don't believe me, and why should you? I know what the people in Enlay think of me. And I know it's not much.'

"He stopped, as if waiting for me to contradict him, but I just kept rolling my cigarette, there in the sun. I was hoping he'd just go away.

"'You could sell them,' Jack repeated, 'for more than you could dream. Magic, John. Things you can't even imagine.' He picked up the beans from where I'd put them, on the shady side of my bench. He held them out to me, shook them in his palm. Colors flashed off their smooth black skins, flashed off and pulled at the eye. It was as if the greens and reds, the blues and violets—oh, the shades of violet, from a pale, newborn tint to a purple the color of the best red wines—were growing inside the beans and being born in the sunlight.

"Jack saw me watching, saw my eyes following the lights, and he played what he obviously considered his winning card. 'Your mother's a nice lady. Doesn't she deserve better?'

"He waved his arm, and that wave encompassed our house and outbuildings. The house had a decided tilt, everything needed paint, there were boards on the stable with holes chewed through them, and the outhouse didn't bear mention.

"'Rich,' Jack whispered. 'Magic, I swear. All yours. Only seven pieces of gold.'

"'If these beans are so wonderful, why don't you

plant them yourself? Even a lazy lad like you should be willing to do a bit of work to get such wonders.'

"Jack waved his hand through the air, ending the movement with an almost regal flick of his wrist. 'No need, John. None at all. I've become rich enough for ten men.'

"I doubted this. I wasn't ready, though, to pursue Jack's idea of the riches of ten. Instead, I asked, 'Then why the seven pieces of gold?'

"Jack laughed. 'Value for value, John. Something for something.'

"Well, happens that I had seven pieces of gold. And a bit more. My last trip had been a profitable one.

"I know what you're thinking. Why not take that gold and do what needed to be done? Fix everything up and probably still have a bit left over on the other side. You're also probably aware that I did nothing of the sort. Instead, I watched those lights flash. I reached out and took those beans. I dipped into my pouch and gave over seven gold coins. And the beans snuggled into my palm like little piggies snuggling into their mother.

"'Just plant them,' Jack said as he pocketed his money, 'and you'll have more to sell than you'll be able to carry, plus magic besides.' And, clearly pleased with himself, Jack went whistling off down the road.

"It was hard to plant those beans. My hand didn't want to give them up. I sat and held them and watched them for the longest time, thrilled by the colors, loving the feeling of them against my skin. Finally I sighed, got up, and dug three small holes in the sunniest spot of my mother's herb garden. I dropped one bean into each hole, although letting go of them was like prying gold from a dead man's fingers, and I added a bit of water from the rain barrel.

"The next morning, on my way to the necessary, something in the garden caught my eye. In the spot where I'd dropped the beans, there were now plants. Three-inch-high plants, strong and healthy, with the barest touch of shimmering black on the stems. I stood looking at them for so long, I almost forgot why I was outside in the first place.

"By that afternoon, those plants were three feet tall. The leaves were glossy and flowers were popping out everywhere. Purple flowers, with mouths like snapdragons. I touched one and felt its warmth; squeezed its sides. It looked like a tiny lion yawning.

"My mother had noticed by now. How could she not? There were aliens in her garden.

"'John? Where did these come from?' She'd spoken from behind me, and I must have jumped a good six inches.

"When my heart returned to normal, I mumbled, 'Lazy Jack.'

"Mumbling didn't work. She heard me.

"'Lazy Jack?' she cried. 'Oh, John, I hope you didn't pay him good money for them. They're sure to be exactly the opposite of whatever he promised.'

"I didn't answer, which was a good enough answer for her. 'Oh, John,' she sighed.

"Since there didn't seem to be anything more to say, we stood shoulder to head (my mother is a tiny thing) and simply looked at the plants. In seven minutes I saw them grow another inch and a half.

"'John?' said my mother. Her voice sounded the way it did when she used to ask me about the girls I'd been seeing, back before she decided she didn't want the details. 'Did those plants just get bigger?'

"'They're supposed to be magic,' I said, which was a rather feeble explanation.

"'Son, don't be ridiculous. You— Oh!' This as the bean plants jumped once again.

"I stepped back a few paces, moving briskly, and said, 'Let's leave them for now. They're probably just fast starters.' I didn't sound convincing, not even to myself.

"But my mother agreed, and together we went back to the house.

"That evening, in the light of a waxing moon, those plants seemed to climb forever. They didn't need stakes, either. They were thick and strong and straight, and I couldn't see the tops no matter how hard I tried.

"By the next morning the little lion blossoms were gone, replaced by the most beautiful rich-purple pods. They glowed with an inner light that we could see just by looking out the windows.

"My mother followed me out of the house, close enough that I could feel her toes against my heels. Christobel, our cat, who had stayed carefully removed from the plant situation until now, walked on my right-hand side. We were all moving slowly, as if we could sneak up on the pods from their blind spots.

"When we were each close enough to touch a plant, I reached out my hand, palm up, and moved it gingerly toward one of the pods. Christobel yowled and bashed her head against my leg. My mother said, 'John, do you think you should?'

"But by now my fingers were touching the pod. Heat radiated off it, heat that I would have sworn I could feel running through my arm all the way up to the elbow. It was the same heat that had come off the beans themselves when Jack had put them in my hand just two days before. I jiggled the pod and watched the color flashes glint in the sun. The reds and blues, the greens, and oh! those violets. I reached for the stem. 'Should I?' I asked.

"Christobel hissed. My mother said, 'Oh, John, I don't know if that's wise.' And the pod fell, snuggling and rolling against my palm like a drowsy little mouse.

"'Well,' I said, but I don't remember what I planned to say after that, because suddenly pods from all three plants began to fall. The three of us—my mother, Christobel, and I—were caught in a rain of pods. By the time the stalks were empty, the herb garden was covered with piles of pods and beans that reached to my knees.

"The falling pods had made a noise like hundreds of fingertips tapping on cloth-covered tables. When they were all off the plants, the silence seemed to echo.

"'Gracious,' my mother finally said. She sounded breathless. 'Goodness gracious.'

"Christobel meowed.

"More silence, until my mother said, 'I'll just go and get a nice basket,' which made me laugh out loud.

"'That's like cleaning up after the flood last spring with a teaspoon.'

"'And what do you suggest?' My mother used her huffy voice.

"I laughed again, and shrugged at the same time. 'I don't really know.'

"'We have to do something. We can't just let them rot.'

"Christobel yowled in agreement.

"'I suppose,' I finally said, 'we could ask the miller

for some of his grain baskets. Just so we could move them into the old barn.'

"'An excellent idea.'

"I hooked up our pony cart, drove toward town, and borrowed baskets from the miller. We worked like dray horses, even Christobel, although her idea of help was to slap both beans and pods out of the baskets after we'd put them in. We eventually filled our whole barn and half of our stable before we were able to take those baskets back.

"We were in the middle of this work when Lazy Jack came back. His eyes widened when he saw our harvest. I stopped shoveling beans long enough to grab him by the arm. 'Jack,' I said, and I smiled my most unpleasant smile. 'Where did these beans come from?'

"'I said they were magic,' Jack said, pulling against me and edging toward the road.

"'You did,' I agreed, following along. 'But you never

said from where.' My mother, who is quite fierce when she chooses to be, was at this moment hidden behind a pile of beans. But Christobel and I were a match for Jack even without her. I gripped his arm tighter and glared down at him. Christobel tried to bite through his shoe. I said, 'Where, Jack?'

"'The—the giant,' Jack stuttered.

"'What giant?' I shook his arm, not gently.

"'The one up there.' Jack pointed straight to the billowy summer clouds, straight to the one that was shaped like a very large dog.

"'A giant in the clouds? That's who gave them to you?'

"Remember that until after I planted Jack's beans, I was unconvinced of magic. While my opinion had changed, I still wasn't sure that I could make the leap required to believe in giants.

"Jack squirmed.

"'Jack?' I asked, squeezing his arm now.

"'Of course. The giant gave them to me. Absolutely. Certainly. He said—'

"There was a roar from over our heads. My grip on Jack's arm slipped, he tried to run, Christobel tangled through his feet, and he skidded into a pile of beans.

"'He STOLE!' roared the voice above our heads. 'Snuck into my house and STOLE, he did.'

"Jack cowered in his pile of beans. 'I never did.' But his voice was a whisper, and he shivered in the hot sun.

"Fine. I believed in giants. And I believed this particular giant much more than I believed Jack. I didn't think I could do anything about Jack's transgressions, but I asked anyway. 'Do you still have what you took?'

"'You believe him?'

"I looked at Jack with contempt. 'Yes, Jack. Of course I do. How else could you have come to have his beans? But you must have taken something else. I doubt even a giant would be this upset about beans.'

"My mother, having joined us, said, 'Oh, Jack. Your poor, poor mother. To have raised a thief for a son.'

"I raised my voice. 'What did he take, Giant?'

"'He took my golden goose, my Jezebel. If I could only get my Jezebel home, I'd forgive and forget.'

"'Jack?'

"But he was gone.

"My legs are long and I move quickly. I had Jack down on the ground before he'd gone a quarter of a league down the road.

"'Jezebel?' I asked.

"Jack was as surly as a bad child when he said, 'At my house.'

"'Not for long,' I said.

"We were back soon enough, standing at the base of the tallest stalk. It was already beginning to shrivel.

"'Giant,' I called, 'your Jezebel is here.' And as I

looked at the goose and the dying beanstalks, I said, 'But I have no idea of how to return her.' I turned to Jack and said, 'How did you get this goose in the first place?'

"'Climbed.' And Jack sneered at me.

"'When you gave me these beans, you didn't think I'd climb up myself? Find the giant and take what was his, like you did?'

"Jack snorted a laugh. 'You? Never. You're too honest.'

"'Honest is as honest does,' my mother said. Jack shrugged and yawned.

"I shook my head in disgust, then looked up the shriveling stalk in front of me. I still couldn't see the top. But I could see that the leaf stems, if followed properly, would form steps, almost like a ladder.

"I turned back to Jack, scanned him from head to toe. I blinked several times to make sure he was really what I was seeing. It was still Lazy Jack, and I was impressed in spite of myself. 'You climbed something like *that*?' I asked.

"Jack straightened his shoulders, and now he grinned, looking quite cocky. 'Of course I did. Where do you think I got the beans in the first place?' He gave a little shrug, still grinning. 'Nothing to it.'

"I stared at the stalk again, pictured climbing up one-handed, and swallowed hard. 'Should I?' I asked. I have never liked high places. I even got scared in the loft of our barn.

"My mother didn't hesitate. 'Of course you should, John. You must. Poor things. They need to be together.' And she gave Jezebel a little pat.

"'Umm. *You* wouldn't want to return her, Mother, would you?'

"'Oh, John. At my age?'

"I gulped and glared at Jack, who had put me in this miserable position. I wouldn't trust him to do it, even if he volunteered. I sighed, then yelled, 'Well then, here we come!' I put my shaking left foot on a stem and grabbed the stalk with my damp right hand. To Jezebel, the goose nestled in my left arm, I said, 'Do not move,' and I started up.

"The stalk that had been so alive yesterday, so supple in the morning, was dry and brittle. Some leaf stems gave off crackling noises, even though I was moving as lightly as possible. I didn't look up, I didn't look down, I just climbed, trying to breathe slow, full breaths between my steps. Jezebel, bless her, stayed quiet, curling into me as if she were nesting in a pile of straw. I could hear Christobel howling below me. And then my head went into the dog cloud and there, in front of my nose, was a shoe the size of one of the miller's baskets.

"I stopped and looked up. Far, far above me was the head of a giant. And reaching toward me was a hand the size of my mother's best dinner platter.

"I decided then that falling, even falling that

terrible long distance, was better than having this huge hand, its meaty fingers decked with silver rings, coming straight toward my face, blotting out the sun. I closed my eyes, let go, and waited for the sensation of tumbling through space, waited for the crash as my body hit the ground.

"But before I fell through the dog cloud, I was grabbed. Now I was swinging free, held in a grasp that was both strong and somehow comforting. I opened my eyes, and there, in front of me, was the giant's face. The one eye I could focus on was the purple shade of spring violets, and there were wrinkles of what looked like concern showing in the corner. With the part of my mind that was still thinking, I realized that I was no longer holding Jezebel. Then one wing flapped and she settled herself, safe on the giant's shoulder.

"'You were about to fall,' said the giant, and he must have known the effect he was having on me, because his voice was as delicate as a giant's voice could be.

"'I don't care for heights,' I managed to gasp, and my own voice was rough and raspy with fear.

"The giant nodded, but all he said was 'I'm just going to place you on this cloud. Until you get your bearings.'

"Now, you may think a cloud would be something you would fall right through. And that was my first thought. I saw myself spinning down once again, saw the ground rising to meet me. But what choice did I have? I was, remember, being held from harm only by the good graces of a giant. I let him put me on the cloud. And when I could breathe again, when I could draw slow, steady breaths, I realized that I wasn't going anywhere at all. I even tapped my right foot, twice. The cloud bounced a bit—rather like a dog shifting his back, waiting for scratches—and that was that.

"A slow smile spread across my face. I looked up

and up once again and I said, 'Thank you, Giant.'

"'Pierre,' he said.

"'Pierre?'

"He nodded.

'I said, 'John,' and I held out my hand. He leaned down, Jezebel shifted her weight on his shoulder, and we shook. Or, more accurately, I put my whole hand around his thumb.

"'It's a good piece of work you've done, sir,' Pierre said. 'And I promise you'll be well rewarded. But I'd like to suggest that you climb back down now. Quickly. Beanstalks don't last forever, you know.'

"As he said this, I noticed that the stem poking through the cloud was beginning to sway. I heard creakings, cracklings, and moans that sounded ominous.

"I moved with a speed I didn't know I possessed. For every three feet I climbed down, I felt two feet of the stalk above me sag and wilt. Perhaps it was some magic from

Pierre, but my feet found footholds where there should have been none. I seemed to have eyes in the soles of my shoes. Until, of course, the last four feet.

"I could blame it on the fact that I was now surrounded by wilting leaves, that I felt as if I were in a particularly dense forest, that my vision was reduced to fading green, but, in the end, I think my luck just gave out. I lost my grip and tumbled the last four feet, eyes closed, mouth open, not sure whether I should scream or not. I knew I was going to land in the worst possible way, was going to break my back or my neck or, at the very least, my leg.

"Instead, I landed on a pile of fallen leaves, a pile so thick, it was like falling onto my own bed covered with our best down quilt. I stayed there for a moment, staring into the sky, searching for broken things on my body. Above me, the dog cloud changed shape and became a castle—drawbridge, moat, and all.

"Then my mother was standing next to me and

Christobel was bashing her head against mine. My mother said, 'Oh, John, are you all right?'

"I'd finished my inventory and had to admit that yes, I was. She smiled and said, 'A man and his goose. That's as it should be.'

"I eyed what was left of my stalk. It was leaning closer and closer to our barn. Then I looked at the others and saw that they were listing even more. Christobel yowled and smacked me in the leg, and I jumped up. My arm brushed against my stalk, which trembled.

"'Run!' my mother cried, and we ran like fury—Jack, Christobel, my mother, and I. When we were at what seemed like a safe distance, we all turned and watched as the last bit of my climbing stalk and what was left of the other two wobbled like drunken men making their various ways home after a night at the local inn. When they crashed into the ground, the earth shook like a quake, and all four of us stumbled. The stalks lay like the dead things they were, inches from the south wall of our barn.

"I was still staring at them when I heard my mother shout, 'Jack! Come back here at once!'

"'Oh, let him go,' I said, contempt in my voice. I didn't even bother to watch Jack's retreat. 'Whatever you want him for, he won't do it. If we're lucky, we'll never see him again. Stealing from a giant.'

"'Young man.' The voice came from above, from the cloud that now looked like nothing so much as a big-nosed smiling face in profile. A face like Pierre's. 'For you. With my thanks.'

"Gold coins began tumbling through the air, spinning and casting sun rainbows on their way to the ground. Coins that equaled the seven I'd given Jack, times seven. When I picked one of them up, it was warm to the touch, warm as the beans had been just two days before. On one side was a striking likeness of Jezebel. On the other, a fully bloomed rose glowed red-gold.

"My mother, looking around my shoulder, gasped. Christobel walked over the dead stalks and swatted at the scattered coins. One last coin tumbled down and landed square in my palm. Instead of Jezebel, this one had a portrait of a woman with thick, long hair, standing next to a large dog. I looked at the gold in my hand and at my feet, looked at the bushels of beans all around me. We had food and we had money. Enough for a long, long time.

"I called up to the sky. 'My thanks to you, Pierre. The best of luck. And don't worry. I won't ever sell your beans.'

"I turned to my mother and said, 'I think, tonight, I'll move my bed up to the sleeping loft.'

"'Why, John,' she said, 'you won't be afraid of the height?'

"I looked up into the sky and said, 'Not anymore.'

"I heard a rumble of thunder that sounded like a chuckle. When I looked up, the sky was the clear blue of the town pond on the first sunny day of spring, and there were no clouds at all."

※

Mama Inez chuckles herself, low in her throat. As Toby accompanies John back to the waiting area, she tosses John's coin back to him, and he catches it with a practiced hand. She stands very still and checks the spin of the world. She can feel the start of the shift back to equilibrium, and she breathes out in relief. It's working, this gathering.

When she looks for the twins, Mama Inez finds them sitting close together, holding hands and having what could be considered a discussion.

"Remember, Earl. You only help if I forget my place."

Earl holds up both hands. "I swear. Only if you forget your place, need local color, or faint."

"Earl! That covers all the time! I'll forget everything. I always do when we both try to speak."

"Oh, please. It's not as if I'll be telling a different story on top of yours."

"You're most distracting, Earl. You always bring in peripherals that turn me sideways."

"Ah. It's your lack of concentration, not my storytelling, that's the problem. Truly."

This last word is half laughed, half yelped, as Earl dodges Maddie's deep-purple tasseled hat, thrown with remarkable accuracy by its owner.

Maddie sighs.

"The story will sound wonderful. You're just nervous, you know," Earl says.

"You're right. Of course you're right."

Earl nods. "Now, deep breath."

Maddie breathes.

"Three more times," says Earl.

She's steadier now.

Mama Inez says, "Ready?" and Maddie sighs again and wrinkles her nose in a way that means she's worried as well as nervous and scared.

But . . . "Come along, then," says Earl. "I'll only be supporting, I'll only interrupt when necessary, and I'll only correct you when you're completely wrong."

"Somehow that isn't very encouraging."

This makes Mama Inez laugh, a growly laugh that comes straight from the belly. That laugh makes Maddie smile. It makes Earl throw his arm around Maddie's shoulders. They walk, linked, out to the teller's cushion.

Lost

"My brother and I are as near identical as twins can be when one is a boy and one is a girl. My name is Madeline, although my brother insists on calling me Maddie. In return, for some small measure of retribution, I call him Earl. As that is not even close to Nathaniel, his true name, and as it irritates him just enough, it seems fair payback."

"Oh, Maddie. Must you do the name story yet again?

"Stop the 'Maddie' and we'll see."

"Maddie, Maddie, tall, thin, and catty."

"I could tell them the Earl rhyme."

"I beg you, lady, no."

"Then may I proceed?"

"Of course."

"You're quite gracious, Earl."

By now the audience has caught the spirit of the twins, the give-and-take, the call and response. The crowd waits, smiling, for whatever will come next.

"If you've not guessed by now, if the points on our ears haven't made it clear, we're elves. But we're far away from the denizens of Faerie, and loyalty to certain humans as well as a sense of adventure keeps us away.

"We were separated from the others by chance."

"No! By exploration."

"True, Earl. And by exploration. We were often accused of digging too much into the world of humans, but it's been our passion since we learned to walk."

"And talk."

"As Earl says. Our caravan was passing by a most charming town. We had spent the night on the fringes, as we were seldom welcomed anywhere we landed. Think of us as Gypsy Travelers. We share their reputation for scrounging, and it's mostly a well-deserved one. Many of those we caravanned with had no problem 'borrowing' whatever they needed from those who made an honest living."

"But not us or our family, Maddie. Don't let them think that. Remember how one of the first lessons we learned at our mother's knee was that ours was ours and theirs was theirs."

"True. But also true, we needed a group to belong to. Moving through the countryside alone was always dangerous. And moving was what we did.

"Before the morning oatmeal was served, Earl and I were out and about. Because our people never stay in any one place for long, we needed to see everything, to experience all of it, before we were pulled on our way. The clean cobbles of the village streets, the sun riding on the thatched roofs, the warm smells of fresh bread—all of this was almost more than we could bear."

"We were fifteen, and for us everything held a sense of wonder, a sense of excitement. We always felt we had to be smack in the middle of it—whatever it was."

"We were gone before our mother could miss us, gone into the cool, fresh damp of morning."

"Gone, with every intention of coming home before the caravan pulled horse stakes, before the wagons were packed, before everything disappeared."

"Earl makes this sound exciting. But being un-welcome in most places is hard."

"No, adventurous. Moving was in our blood."

"Although it could be sad."

"Well, yes. But on this day—"

"On this day the whole world seemed welcoming,

as if it had been put together just for our benefit. The sky was the perfect shade of blue that only seems to show in the early morning, the birds were singing the summer in, the river danced with water sprites, and, in the center of all this, the town smiled and held out its arms. It was—"

"Irresistible."

"We wandered the town. We bought a loaf of smooth bread from the baker, bottles of mead from the vintner, green-and-gold pears that were just ripe enough to make the juices drip down our chins. We stopped in the square, sat on the lime-green grass, and watched the pageant of life parade past us. A coconut-brown dog joined us, and we fed him bits and pieces of our picnic."

"But we misjudged."

"'Misjudged.' A nice word. A polite word. An untrue word. We made a huge and very complete mistake. We've lived with it ever since."

"You make it sound terrible. Threatening."

"Not at all."

"It hasn't been terrible, Maddie. In its own way, it's been very fine."

"In its own way."

"When we went back to join the caravan, it was gone."

"We can make things vanish. We're fey, after all."

"But Maddie, no one had ever made the caravan vanish."

"I never said. I only made a cogent comment."

"Just tell, Maddie."

"While our caravan hadn't been spelled away, there was certainly a spell that cloaked its direction of travel. And a good, strong spell at that. We stood in the empty field that had been so full of life the night before. We sent out feelers, floating our searches on the four winds. And we found nothing."

"We were fifteen, remember. In fact, we're barely

sixteen now. For an elf, that's very young. Our finding powers were still quite weak."

"We were on our own for the first time. It was an adventure. No one to report to. No explanations for any behavior, no matter how peculiar. No schedules. Bedtime whenever we chose. Then the seasons began to move through their cycles. Summer skidded into autumn. We cavorted through town, keeping below the radar of the humans."

"Which is quite easy for an elf."

"That sounds so much like bragging, Earl."

"It's not. It's truth. It's only hard to hide when you're in a group, like our old caravan. Now tell them about the part when things began to stumble."

"We had no way to get back to our caravan. We had long ago run out of money. During the warm months, we had been reduced to 'borrowing' food and drink. Sleeping under the stars had been fun. And on rainy or thunderous nights, we'd slip into dry sheds or the upper reaches of stables. The brown dog from the square always seemed to know when we were unsure of our next move. He'd appear like he had magic of his own, to guide us. He knew every hidey-hole in town.

"Then autumn skidded into winter. Our adventure rapidly became less wonderful. We decided, after a miserable night of cold during the first snow, that we needed a permanent place to call our own.

"The next day, chilled and bedraggled, we walked up and down the main street of our adopted village. We looked in all the windows, remember, Earl? We listened at all the doors. We stopped at the shoemaker's. We knew he was a shoemaker from our earlier, carefree wanderings, when finding a home had been of no importance. We were sure that we knew everything about everyone in the village. We observed without being observed ourselves. But had we not known how this man made his living, we would have found it out only by the conversation we heard through the keyhole of the garden door. There was nothing in his street window to indicate a trade."

"The window was, in fact, completely empty."

"The shop was unhappy."

"As were its inhabitants. They were saying . . . No. You tell, Maddie. You do it so much better than I."

"Earl. How kind."

"I always am."

"The shoemaker and his wife were saying they had nothing left. The new shoemaker, to the north and across the square, had taken all their business with his fancy shoes made with polished leathers. Our shoemaker made working shoes, sturdy and long lasting, but suddenly everyone needed to look as if they were going to town, going to the palace, going to a ball. No one, it seemed, had the money left over for strong, simple shoes.

"The shoemaker held up a piece of golden leather."

"We saw, through the keyhole."

"He told his wife that it was the last piece he had. Tonight he would cut his last pair of shoes, tomorrow he would make them, then heaven alone knew what would happen."

"Don't forget, Maddie and I watched. And we remembered what we saw. We knew, for example, that the barber was not at all kind to his wife or to his children."

"We knew that the vintner drank more of his product than he sold."

"We knew the new shoemaker, the one who called himself a cobbler, used old leather and colored it the shades of the rainbow to disguise its poor condition. We knew his dyes would fade quickly. We knew he used one stitch when he should have used three. And that his soles were thin and slippery."

"As was his soul, actually."

"Earl! A metaphor."

"We knew good things, too. We knew our shoe-maker spent long hours on his shoes, charged as little as possible, believed devoutly in the power of a good pair of shoes to smooth out a day."

"We listened, and the brown dog listened with us. Then he shoved us closer to the door with his dark coconut-brown head. 'Do you want us to go in?' I asked. He didn't bark, seeming to know our need for stealth, but he did nod his head.

"Earl said, 'We do need someplace to sleep.'

"I said, 'We could help.'

"That night, when the shoemaker and his wife had gone to bed, we magicked his door lock and crept into his workroom. The golden leather was cut, ready to be stitched. It was going to make a beautiful pair of brogues.

"We pieced the leathers together, Earl and I. We stitched the leathers to the soles with stitches so fine, no human would ever have been able to match them.

Not even our shoemaker."

"And certainly not the cobbler to the north."

"We added decorative accents. Embossed leaves around the lace holes. We polished the leather until it shone like fresh coins. Then, just as the sun was cresting, we climbed the narrow ladder stairs to the attic. We'd made shoes for the shoemaker and found a place to stay for us. An even trade. To make sure he saw things as we did, to make sure he appreciated our part of the bargain, we eavesdropped."

"When the shoemaker and his wife woke early the next morning, he said, and I quote, 'Sweet heaven, my Mary. Look at these shoes. I've never seen any as fine. Did you do this while I lay sleeping?'"

"Earl! That sounds just like our shoemaker. Well done!"

"Thank you. Mary, of course, denied having anything to do with the shoes."

"Knowing that somehow he'd had an amazing

piece of luck as good as handed to him, the shoemaker put the golden shoes in his empty shop window. 'If we sell them, Mary, we'll eat for at least another week,' he said.

"Pleased with ourselves, feeling that our part of the bargain had been paid, even if the shoemaker wasn't aware of our trade, Earl and I fell asleep, curled like field mice in the warm, sweet-smelling attic.

"An hour later, well before the start of the business day, when the sun was barely pushing against the cracks in the attic walls, a battering at the street door woke us.

"'Those shoes in your window!' a man cried. 'They're beautiful. I must have them.'

"Our shoemaker agreed that they were indeed beautiful.

"'Please let me try them on. I only hope they fit as well as they look. I really must have them!'

"When the man tried the shoes on, they fit as if

they'd been custom-made for his feet alone."

"Elven magic. In the stitching."

"The man sighed with delight and purchased the shoes for a sum that made us gasp."

"It's always nice to see one's work appreciated, don't you think, Maddie?"

"The thing we'd hoped for had come to pass. We now felt completely confident that we'd worked to pay for the roof under which we had rested our heads. One good deed means another will follow."

"Do unto others."

"And we did so need a place to stay."

"So stay we did. We fell back asleep, pleased with ourselves and our new home.

"We did the same good deed the next night. And again. And again."

"It's wise to keep your goodness in the plus column."

"Each night, the shoemaker cut the leather he'd

purchased with that day's sales. Often there were one or two—"

"Or three!"

"—more pairs than had been there the day before. But the leather was always the finest available. The cuts were always well done, the designs both practical and imaginative. Our rival to the north soon had a show window filled with nothing but faded leather, shadows, and dust. Remember the dust, Earl?

"Then, one night when the winds were particularly fierce, when our attic shook like a ship lost at sea, we found clothing mixed among the leathers."

"The most warm and comfortable clothes."

"Yes. Oh, Earl, remember the sweater? The one with the flock of sheep playing in the spring fields?"

"How could I forget? You grabbed it almost before I saw it. In fact, all I could see, that night, were the colors. Pale green, white, and robin's-egg blue. In all probability it was meant for you all along."

"I loved that sweater."

"Which is why you love the winter so, I imagine. I myself was especially pleased with the pants. The right size. Even for my long legs."

"We pranced like children in our new clothes. We almost forgot the shoes. When we remembered, we worked like demons. We stitched the red boots, nailed the blue slippers, laced the rich brown brogues. We finished just as the sun was showing its face over the village green."

"Which was when we heard the creak on the stairs. We whirled around, but there was nothing there to see."

"*You* didn't see anything, Earl. *I* saw a slippered foot and the trailing hem of a nightshirt."

"Perhaps."

"Oh, Earl. Certainly I did. And it made us talk that day in our little attic space. We had the clothes. Proof that someone was watching us as we were watching them. Didn't it follow, then, that they approved of us? It was a thought that was both alarming and appealing."

"Generally, our people are told to get along, move along, no stopping, no standing."

"To get approval, even a somewhat sideways approval, was a rare thing. A thing to be treasured."

"I know that I worked twice as hard after that."

"We finally had a chance to test our approval theory. When Earl became so hot with the fever that I was afraid his body would burn through the attic floor, I went downstairs in the light of day.

"The shoemaker's Mary started when she saw me, then approached me with caution, as one would approach a wild thing. But I was past being wild. I just needed someone to help with my brother.

"'Please,' I begged, and before I'd even finished telling her of Earl, Mary was negotiating the attic steps, an earthen bowl of cold well water laced with tincture of rosemary in her hands. I followed behind, carrying a stack of soft, clean cloths.

"Mary brushed the hair off Earl's hot face. Her fingers found the points on his ears.

"'Elves,' she said, and for a moment her hands stopped moving. 'We didn't know it was elves we saw that night when we hid on the stairs. We only thought it was children.' She paused, then said, almost to herself, 'Although we did wonder how children could do that kind of cobbler work.

"My heart began to beat in my throat. She knew what we were. She'd push us away. We'd be judged on the reputation of our kind, not on the work we'd done."

"Which just shows how addled her brain was. Almost as addled as my own."

" 'Oh, please,' I begged again. 'We're not like the others. Please don't tell us to get along, move along. Not now.'

"Mary looked at me, her gray eyes steady. She dipped a cloth into the well water and pressed it to Earl's forehead. She draped a second one across his left wrist.

"'Child,' she said clearly, 'you're welcome to stay as long as you like. Both of you.'"

"And stay we did. She pulled me through, did Mary. She and the shoemaker."

"Wonderful Mary. Wonderful shoemaker. We've been there ever since."

❧

The twins are almost dancing with excitement when they've finished their story.

"Did you see? Did you feel?" Maddie cries in happiness as they cross the threshold into the waiting area. "They liked it. They liked it as well as all the other tales they've heard tonight!"

"As well?" Earl asks. "I think they may have liked it the best."

"Nicely told," says John as they bounce past him.

"Oh, thank you," Maddie sings. "Yours, too. Wonderful." And she giggles in pure happiness.

Toby steps up to the twins and smiles a dog smile. Both Earl and Maddie stop, look at Toby, look at each other, and say, "Oh," on a long breath.

"It was you, wasn't it?" Maddie says, kneeling down to hug the dog.

Toby barks once. He touches Earl's foot with his paw and wanders through the crowd of storytellers before he joins Mama Inez.

"A magic all his own," Earl says as he watches Toby.

Toby smiles his dog smile at Mama Inez. She reaches down and rubs his ears. "Excellent work, my boy," she says as she remembers how Toby found the twins' story by himself. A leaf the color of maple syrup had landed near the waterfall just as she was getting ready to slide into Mae's story; Mae, who hadn't been able to come to this gathering. Toby had barked three times.

"I know," Mama Inez had said in a distracted way, "but I can't. Not now."

Toby had simply nodded his big head, turned sideways, and slipped away.

Now Mama Inez ruffles his fur and repeats, "Excellent work. A perfect addition to tonight's gathering."

Toby bows, gracious as royalty. He turns to his left, and there's Maisie.

To both Mama Inez and Toby she says, "I thought I knew something about magic. I thought I'd seen all of it that existed in this world." She laughs and shakes her head. "I'm not even close, am I? Look at all of us. You can drink the magic floating through this room, like the best wine."

Mama Inez agrees. "It's always amazing. I've

seen it before, but each time it's completely different."

"It's hard for me to imagine that it was ever this strong. But then I used to think magic was only fey folk watching our goats."

"Things change all the time," Mama Inez says. Lights flash in her eyes, and for the hint of a second Maisie sees the ripple of the water in the Mile River on a fall night. Maisie blinks, looks again, and sees the ripple once more, which makes her know that she and Mama Inez have met before. She says, simply, "Thank you."

"You're most welcome," Mama Inez says with a smile.

Maisie thinks about magic and change, how they both can come when you least expect it. Then she thinks about the reason for tonight's gathering. "And the stumble in the world. Are we having an effect?"

Mama Inez stands, quiet, contemplative, her fingers curled in Toby's fur. She reaches out to touch the world with all her senses, to feel the spin. In her mind she pulls on the story strands. Her fingers dance on a spindle only she can see as she spins the wool of tonight's stories, then twists it in with other patterns of the universe. After a moment, Mama Inez breathes out a long, gentle breath. Halfway there, is what she thinks. Half the way to correcting the spin, to healing the ripple. She's able to tell Maisie, with certainty, "We're well on the way," which makes Maisie nod and step out to the teller's cushion with a confident stride.

Mama Inez and Toby walk to the back of the tent. Here Mama Inez arranges, in her raku jar, the talismans used so far: the brocade ribbon, the seashell, the gold coin, the tiny purple brogue. She adds Maisie's stone from the Mile River, then goes back to the tent opening to watch and to listen.

The moon is sending just enough light into the tent to glimmer off the cups and glasses of the crowd. In the waiting area, Roberto and Franz move their rings around, weighing shapes, styles, and colors. Maisie sits cross-legged and begins.

Carter House

"EVERYTHING STARTED WHEN I brought up the topic of Carter House. You, too, I'm sure, would be curious if your family lived in a small cottage and kept goats when they also owned a manorish house just over the southern hills. You, too, would ask questions, just as you would want to see the place that, being an only child, would one day belong to you.

"It started at breakfast. 'Father, let's go to Carter House,' I said. 'I'd like to see it. You always promised I'd be able to go when I got older.' I'd stayed away all my life, less because of a desire to mind my parents than because of the reputation of the place, dangerous and decrepit. And because of the nightmare stories I'd heard of the horrible things that happened to people bold enough to go there.

"But the horrible things I heard about always happened at night, and always, of course, on a night when there was no moon, and they were, I was realizing, always described by a friend of a friend. They'd taken on the cast of legend. Still, I'd stayed away. And here I was, eighteen. As I told my father, 'Eighteen today. My birthday. That's old enough, surely.'

"When I got no response, I played my best card. 'It's a beautiful day. We can take a picnic.'

"Really, there's nothing to compare with eating in a sun-drenched glade, breezes in your hair, bird shadows racing across the grass. I knew the weakness both my parents had for picnics.

"My father's answer was short and to the point. 'No,' he said.

"My father is a loquacious man. One of the things he loves to do best is to talk. About everything and nothing.

"'No?' I asked, surprised. 'Just no?'

"'Maisie, let it go,' my mother said. 'No one goes to Carter House.'

"'Then no one will be there to disturb us.'

"My father, a calm man in most circumstances, began to glower. 'Maisie. The answer is no.'

"I looked at both my parents. My mother, uncharacteristically, said nothing and twisted her hands. My father was agitated. His own hands fluttered over the breakfast things, two lost doves looking for a resting place.

"I was in the middle of deciding if I should press my point when my mother came to a decision. I knew because she relaxed her hands, shifted her weight in a way that made me remember that she was descended from royalty, and said, on a soft sigh, 'Oh, tell her, Peter. It's time.'

"My father looked angry, but my mother had made up her mind. When this happens, there's no stopping her. 'She has a right to know. She may even have a need.' Then she repeated, 'It's time.'

"He seemed to deflate, to fold in on himself like a house built of soft, old cards. 'Haunted,' he whispered in a voice like the winds blowing across the low marsh grasses. 'Haunted and wrapped in fey spells. That means danger.'

"'Haunted.' 'Fey.' 'Danger.' Which should come first? 'What sort of danger?' I asked.

"'The kind that hurts mortals. Never, Maisie, never get involved with the fey.'

"Ah. He'd given me two words for one. I preened, proud of my choice. I wanted to capture 'haunted' next, but that short little word 'fey' was standing in my way.

"'Wait. You've always said the fey are on our side. They help with the goats, you've said, keep them giving milk, keep them strong and healthy. Isn't that why we put out the cakes and the coffee? As offerings?'

"'Yes, of course,' my mother said. 'Your father only meant to stay away from the fey at Carter House. There are fey and there are fey, my daughter.'

"'Could you be a bit more obscure? I'm almost understanding you.' I watched my parents. They watched me until my father's gaze faltered and he sighed, another low, mournful sound.

"'You could just tell me,' I suggested. 'I'm an adult now.'

"'Peter,' my mother said, and she sounded as if she were encouraging him.

"He sighed again, but this time the sigh merged with his story. 'Almost twenty-one years ago, and still just as painful.' Then, as if he'd had a flash of inspiration, he said, 'You could tell, Marigold.'

"'It's not my story,' she said, her emphasis on 'my.'

"My father took a long drink from his coffee cup, then made a face. 'Cold,' he whined.

"There was a warning look in my mother's eyes

as she rose and said, 'I'll make a fresh pot. You have a story to tell.'

"He watched her walk away and kept his eyes on the doorway even after she'd disappeared. I cleared my throat. He turned back to me and said with great reluctance, 'He was my best friend, you see. We'd known each other all our lives. We played at being warriors, even though we'd been lucky enough to never see a war. We acted rough and worldly, even though we'd never been farther than the outskirts of town. We dreamed of honor and glory. And then he—he was lost.'

"'Who was lost?'

"'Thom, of course,' my father said, surprise in his voice. 'Thom Lyndenhall, the one who haunts Carter House.'

"This wasn't going to be easy. 'Thom was your friend?' I tried.

"A nod from my father.

"'He was lost at Carter House?'

"'My father's house, yes, and my home. Thom visited so often, he had his own room.'

"I shook my head. 'I'm sorry, I don't understand.'

"'Eighteen is a dangerous age.' My father looked straight at me, and now his gaze was sharp and focused. 'Eighteen is when you know you rule the world, when you believe everything and everyone will bow down before you.'

"I was indignant. 'I don't—'

"He went right on. 'Eighteen was what we were when we went out on that full-moon Halloween night. Our shadows ghosted before us while we waited to see if the Queen of the Faeries really rode at midnight, when the line between real and magic is so thin, it can be broken by a light puff of wind.'

"I remembered all my parents' warnings, repeated yearly, about never being away from home after dark on Halloween. I pictured two young men, bold and brash, casting hollow moon shadows and waiting for the queen.

"'And did the queen ride?' I asked.

"'Oh, yes. She and her entire entourage. We heard them coming from far away. You know how sound carries when the night is still and cold. We heard the hoofbeats, the jangle of bridles decked with bells. Then we saw them, their shadows stretching before them, long and thin, and as ghostly as our own.

"'When they actually appeared, the queen rode at the front, on a horse as black as the night itself. She was dressed in green, the color of new spring grass. Behind her came what must have been her high court, all on horses of brown in shades ranging from bitter chocolate to cocoa. At the back was the white horse, just the one. White as our goat's best cream. And on that white horse's back, collared with garlands of spring flowers—'

"'Wait, wait,' I interrupted. 'Spring flowers? On Halloween?'

"My father kept his eyes on my face and nodded, one short, emphatic nod. 'The same thing Thom said.

"'"Peter," he whispered. "Lily of the valley. Jack in the pulpit. Purple hyacinth. Tooth of the lion." And "Shhh," I told him. "Shush. Quiet."

"'I spoke as softly as I could, but it was no use. She'd heard his voice.

"'We saw her double back, did Thom and I. Heard her asking her court who was lurking in the bushes. And Thom shoved at me, knocked me down to hide me, just before she was upon us.'

"'And?' I asked, urgent. Because it was coming, I knew it was. Something horrible was here, and I needed to know what it was, what my father had been so reluctant to reveal for all these years.

"'And I scrambled away on my hands and knees until I could get up and run.' It was the barest whisper. 'And Thom has not been seen for these twenty-one years.'

"I sat, stunned, and stared at my father.

"'You left him there?' My voice sounded rusted and scratchy.

"'I did,' my father said, 'and I've regretted it ever since.'

"'This is why we've never been to Carter House?'

"It was my mother who answered—answered so quickly, she must have been listening just out of sight to the whole story.

"'When Thom disappeared, it was just after your father began courting me. Within three and a half years, everything at Carter House came to a halt. Crops. Animals. It all seemed to wind down like a broken clock. No one knew why. Nothing anyone tried helped. And by then, we had you to consider.'

"'So you came here?' I waved a vague hand that stirred dust motes in the air and sent them skidding into the corners of our cottage.

"'We did.' My mother's voice was calm and proud.

She came and stood next to my father, rested a hand on his shoulder. 'And we've been happy here. We've done well enough. We've even prospered.'

"I read the spaces between her words. 'You miss it,' I said in surprise. 'The manor house. The grounds. Space to walk without having to dance jigs around each other. You miss it all.'

"'I could stay here easily, and die happy,' my mother said, 'but yes, there are times when I do miss it.'

"My father looked at her, and that look was so sad that I made my decision right then. I would go to Carter House. I would win back what belonged to us. I would regain my family's rights and my father's pride.

"I went that very night. There may have been some truth in my father's comments about eighteen-year-olds, after all. When our cottage had relaxed into sleep, I went out under the glow of a thin crescent moon. I followed my lamp's light across the fields to Carter House. It loomed large well before I walked through the gate.

"Twenty steps in stood a fine, strong horse, gray as weathered stone, tied to the broken brick that edged an old well. In the light from my lamp I could see roses tangled around the well winch. Blood roses, and roses as white as my mother's best tablecloths after they've baked in the afternoon sun. I never even thought. I patted the nose of the horse, and I picked two roses, one red, one white.

"By the time I had the roses twined together, using some of the tall grasses that brushed against my boots, he was in front of me. Tall and slender, with cheekbones that caught and held the light, and eyes that held the stars. Looking in those eyes was like falling into the universe.

"There was scorn and anger in his voice when he said, 'You pick my roses.'

"Yes, he was beautiful. But if these roses belonged to anyone, they belonged to me. I let that show in my voice when I said, 'No. I pick *my* roses.'

"He smiled, but there was little humor when he said, 'By what right do you call these yours?'

"'By right of birth. And you?'

"He stammered a bit. 'By birth? But—but I live here.'

"'Ah. You haven't done much with the place, have you?' I looked at the overgrowth, the tangles and brambles, the broken windows gripping pieces of the fingernail moon.

"'Who are you, then?' Bravado.

"'Maisie Carter.' Then I repeated my previous question. 'And you?'

"'Thom Lyndenhall.'

"I know my mouth dropped open. I know my eyes got wide. I even know that I stopped breathing. And when I started breathing and was able to talk, all I could say was 'You can't be.'

"He laughed then. 'Do you say so? But you see,

here I am, and this is me.'

"I sat down, more because my legs felt wobbly than out of any true desire to sit in the damp muddle of grasses. I looked up at him. The skinny moon drew a halo around his head. I said, 'My father's name is Peter Carter.'

"He sat down, too, thumping hard on the ground. 'I once knew a Peter Carter.' He spoke slowly, and his eyes were tight on my face. 'He was my friend. My best friend.'

"I nodded.

"'And this was his house,' he continued.

"I nodded again and pulled at the grass tangles.

"'How old are you?' It was, and was not, an abrupt change of subject.

"'Eighteen. Today.'

"'And you're here now. Which means . . . How long have I been—gone?'

"I swallowed twice, then said, 'If what I hear is

true, twenty-one years.'

"Thom was silent for so long that I thought I saw the moon shift in the sky. When he did finally speak, it was as if he were alone. 'Twenty-one years . . . Ah, Peter. If I'd only gone with you that night.'

"He looked at me then, straight at me. When he spoke this time, he sounded desperate. 'You can't imagine what it's like. As long as the queen is pleased, everything is beautiful. It's a game, a wonderful game. Life passes you by. You never age, or even think about the passage of time. But of course, there's payment for everything.' He waved a hand from his face to his feet. 'Look at me, and think of your father.'

"I looked, and for the first time in my life I thought of age, and youth, and the balance between the two. Was everlasting youth a blessing or a penance? What-ever the answer was, there was still my father and his culpability in all this. 'He ran away. He left you.' I sup-pose I wanted to sound righteous and indignant, but instead I sounded like I was begging Thom to correct my father's tale.

"Thom did just what I was hoping for. He sat up, his back sword straight. 'No, he did not. At least not in the way you suggest. Think of him, Maisie. Is Peter Carter the type who would run?'

"I didn't answer, mostly because I didn't know what to say. I had never before thought of my father as someone who would leave a friend in need, but he himself had said he'd left Thom behind.

"'You know him as a father,' Thom continued. 'I know him as the best friend a man ever had. The queen—she'd already heard my voice. Heaven help me, somehow she even knew my name. I shoved Peter away. She seemed unaware of him, and I made him go. There was no hope for me, you see. Not then, not when she knew about me. And when you're caught in her beauty, when she wants you—well, you want her, too.'

"He hesitated before adding, 'When I shoved him away, it wasn't just to keep him safe, you know. I wanted to be the only one.'

"He seemed to be waiting for a reaction. When I kept my face smooth and blank, he added, 'We both did what we thought was best at the time.' His eyes traveled from my hair to my feet. 'I look at you, and I know who made the better decision. Especially since I have only until Allhallows Eve to try to do something of note with my life. I doubt that I'll be able to manage a thing as fine as you by then.'

"I did react then. I blushed. To cover my feelings of pride and embarrassment, I asked, 'What happens on Allhallows Eve?'

"He laughed, empty and low. 'Surely you know of the tithe?'

"I shook my head.

"'No?' He sounded quite surprised. 'Peter never explained?'

"'He never did.' I didn't bother to add that I'd only learned of Thom's existence this morning.

"Thom nodded. 'It was always more rumor than anything. But as I said, nothing comes for free. It's true for the queen as well. Every seven years, she pays to keep her kingdom. Price—one mortal, soul and all.'

"I winced. 'Nasty.'

"'Most probably.'

"I knew, in a sudden flash of understanding, just what he was saying. I asked anyway. 'We're not speaking in the abstract here, are we?'

"'We are not.'

"I coughed a bit, cleared my throat, and finally said, 'You're the tithe.' This time it wasn't a question.

"'She always grows tired of you, eventually. And her life is so very, very long. I don't think she understands how precious it can all be to a mortal.' He sounded like he was giving something away, something that would offer the queen an easy out.

"'Don't apologize for her,' I said in disbelief.

"'Ah, but she's so easy to apologize for.' He shrugged. 'So beautiful and so . . .'

"'She sounds horrible! Self-centered. Unfeeling. And, may I remind you, she's going to kill you.' I must admit that my voice here was a bit shrill.

"'Well. Not exactly. And even though a killing will most probably take place, it won't come from her own hand.'

"'Oh, please. You don't want to die, but as long as she doesn't do it herself, it's acceptable?'

"Thom shrugged. 'I just don't see another outcome. Believe me, I have been looking.'

"'Let's think about this,' I said. 'She's been paying her tithe for how long?'

"He shrugged again. 'Since the beginning of time?'

"'Are you telling me'—I tried to speak calmly, but I knew I sounded beyond angry—'no one's ever escaped? No one's ever just run away?' I was up now, stomping through the grass tangles. I was chilled from sitting too long in the damp, but I also needed to move, to calm down. 'Everyone just goes along, meek and mild, and says, "Fine, make me your sacrifice, I don't mind"?'

"Thom stood, too, and stopped my pacing by touching my arm. His voice was gentle when he said, 'It's not that easy to just run away. She can find you almost anywhere in this wide world, and seven leagues beyond it, too. On the off chance that she loses you, she'll take, in your place, whomever you hold most dear.'

"I looked at him with wide eyes.

"'Yes,' he agreed. 'Personally, I admit that I want nothing so much as to get out of this. I don't want to die, especially not for her. I also don't want her to go after someone else. Your father, for example.'

"'How would she know?'

"Thom shrugged for a third time. 'She just would. I promise you.'

"'So there's no way out?'

"Thom hesitated, then said, 'From all I've been able to tell, there's one and only one. And I have no real control over it.'

"I waited for several heartbeats before I said, 'Are you going to make me ask?'

"He was almost playful when he said, 'Someone pulls me off a horse.'

"I waited again, waited to hear the rest. Nothing else came. 'That's it?'

"He nodded.

"'And that doesn't count as escaping?'

"'There are rules even she has to follow.'

"'This may be silly,' I said carefully, 'but why don't you just jump off on your own? It's only a horse.'

"Thom snorted, sounding very much like a horse himself. 'Magic.'

"'Oh.' I felt rather stupid. She was the Fey Queen, after all. 'Of course.' I moved doggedly ahead. 'Someone just pulls you off your horse?'

"'There is a bit more,' he said, and then he repeated my 'of course.'

"Wasn't there always, I thought. I was leaning against the well. The night was fading in the east. I'd been here much longer than I'd planned. 'Can you tell the "more" quickly? If my father finds me gone . . .'

"There was a studied nonchalance in his voice that didn't match his words. 'If someone gets me off the horse, I turn into things. I saw it happen once, during a rescue.'

"'Things?'

"He gave the characteristic shrug that he'd been using all evening. 'You know. Things. A lion. A snake. A snapping swan.'

"'Oh, of course. Things like that. I should have known.'

"'Sarcasm?'

"I ignored that and said, 'And?'

"'And the rescuer needs to hold on. If she lets go, the queen's won once again. From what I understand, she almost always does. And then it's all over for me.'

"'The one you watched—she let go?'

"'Didn't make it past the snake.'

"I thought about this for almost a minute. 'It has to be a she?'

"'Ah. No.' In the faint light of the rising sun I could see him blush. 'Not a she. Just a lover.'"

❖❖

"I got home before I was missed, but just barely. I tried every definition of the word 'lover' I could think of as I fed the goats, cleaned their pens, washed and polished the dishes and utensils, chopped, and swept. All definitions made me nervous.

"I had started this by wanting to reclaim a house and the honor of my family name. Now it seemed that I was being called upon to reclaim a life. I was in deeper than I'd expected, and it seemed that I was going to have to go deeper still if I truly wanted to save this man—my father's best friend, long vanished.

"Suddenly I wished I'd never heard of Thom Lyndenhall or Carter House. My wishing didn't make things go away. Something had to be done, and it looked like it was up to me to do it. After all, it was only two weeks until Halloween.

"The next night, I went back. This time I picked no roses. It wasn't necessary. Both he and his horse were standing by the well, looking as if they'd known I was coming, looking as if we'd had this date arranged for weeks.

"'Maisie,' he said.

"'Thom.'

"We were both so very polite, acting as if we were meeting for the first time at a formal-dress party. Then he smiled. My breath slipped and caught in my throat.

In the slow, slanted autumn moonlight, he looked like a true consort for the queen. I could see why she'd wanted him those twenty-one years ago.

"The only thing I couldn't see was why she'd decided to let him go.

"'I've thought about what you said.' I was close to him now, close enough to touch.

"'Have you?'

"I nodded. And then I kissed him, and he kissed back, a deep kiss, full of longing. We finally pulled apart and breathed air into our lungs. I leaned against his warmth and strength, and I said, 'Tell me again, what will you turn into when you're pulled from that horse?'

"We spent the next ten days plotting. He repeated the colors and order of the horses in the queen's procession until I was reciting them in my sleep.

First goes the black,
Then goes the brown,

Then I run to the white steed
And pull Thom right down.

"A little poem he'd written to help me keep everything straight, no matter how scared I became.

"I also memorized the things he might turn into. For this I had no poem. We were guessing at best, based on what he'd seen with his own eyes. Lion. Snapping swan. Adder. And just how, I wondered, did one protect oneself from an adder wrapped in one's arms? Or the teeth of a lion? Or . . .

"I finally came to the obvious conclusion that I would have to deal with things as they came. Forewarned is forearmed, but I could only do so much.

"In between lions and horses, we spent time getting to know each other.

"'Moons about like she's in love,' I heard my father say to my mother one evening. He sounded both astonished and sad.

"My mother said nothing, but she began pressing special bitter-tasting teas into my hands at meals. The winks she gave me along with the teas let me know that she knew just what I might be doing. I blessed her for her understanding.

"I waited until forty-five minutes before midnight on the night of Halloween before I left our cottage. No one tried to stop me. This may have been because of the low-voiced argument I had heard early in the evening, behind my parents' closed bedroom door. I believed my mother was the winner. When I cracked open the front door and slid through like the thinnest sliver of moonlight, I relied on that belief, and the fact that the only words I had heard clearly from their argument had been 'Peter, leave her be!'

"I hid my hair under a loden-green cloak of thick wool, as the night air was turning to frost on the grasses. The moon was thinning in the clear sky. The stars looked like they could cut glass, and the constellations were so brilliant, they looked as if they were planning to come to life as soon as they neared the ground.

"I went to Miles Cross, the crossroads closest to Carter House. Horses, I was assuming, even magic horses, would need roads. This was close to the spot where Thom had first been taken. I hid myself close to the bank of the Mile River. Then I shivered in the frost and the moonlight, and I waited.

"It wasn't that long before I heard the creak and jangle of leather bridles mixed with the jaunty, metallic ringing of bells. In the moonlight and shadows I saw the horses coming, coming in the exact order that Thom had described. First came the black, ebony dappled with starshine. On his back was the most beautiful woman I'd ever seen, tall, slender, ethereal. Her mane of hair reached to her knees and flowed around her like a cloak of shimmering gold.

"Behind her came the court, on horses in all shades

of brown. These people, too, were tall and lovely. And remote. They rode straight-backed, and they looked ahead in a line as straight as their backs. Their eyes never once strayed to the right or the left.

"Finally, at the end of the procession, with more space between him and the court than there had been between the court and the queen, there was Thom. He was astride a horse the color of cold, fresh cream. He was dressed in white silks and leggings the color of new leaves in spring. There was a garland of French lilacs, lily of the valley, rue, purple hyacinth, and lavender around his neck, and a circlet of red-and-white clover around his head. There was a frozen, hopeless kind of smile on his face, and desperation in his eyes.

"I pulled in my breath, squeezed my eyes shut, and crossed my arms and fingers, pleading for strength. As the white horse passed me, I jumped from my hiding place and flung myself at Thom. The horse shied, but I caught Thom's leg just below the knee, wrapped my arms around his calf, and pulled. The horse went one way, and Thom and I went another. Thom came off so easily that I knew he had to be helping as much as he was able.

"We tumbled together, a jumble of arms, legs, bodies, and heads, onto the cold, stiff grass. I felt my green cloak rip. Thom's mouth was close to my ear when he gasped, 'I wasn't sure you'd really come.' I might have tried to answer, but the breath was knocked out of me, and the sound of iron-shod hoofs fading in the distance held all my attention. That is until, to my left, I heard a cry of displeasure from the queen.

"But Thom was still in my arms, half on top of me, still very much a human being. I was finally able to gasp, 'I told you I would,' and was mentally congratulating myself, feeling bruised but proud, when his silks and skin melted into fur, and his slim body turned into a mass of muscles. A roar blew hot breath on my face as I grappled ineptly with a lion. A small lion, but a lion all the same.

"The lion twisted and clawed, and just as I was sure I couldn't hold on for a fraction of a second longer, the shape changed again into something feathered, with enormous wings and a snapping black beak. My harried brain recognized the thing as the second transformation Thom had mentioned, the swan. I tried to hold the neck and the wings both, but as soon as I felt that I had everything caught and held steady, one wing would come up, flapping, or the beak would snap much too close to my face.

"I fought and tried to keep from harming the bird, because if something happened to it, what would happen to Thom? I was already a mass of scratches and bumps, and I was only up to the second transformation. Then the shape changed again. Now it was something long, thick, and hissing, with fangs exposed. Adder, I thought, even as I yelped and shifted my grip. I grabbed the snake around the neck and held that fang-filled mouth as far away from my face as my arms would reach.

"The snake's head bobbed closer. I screamed. Tears were running down my cheeks. I was cold and wet, but here I was, up to the third thing, and Thom hadn't said a word about anything else. If I could just hold on a bit longer . . .

"Which was, of course, when Thom changed again. The snake disappeared, and I was clutching a burning brand of iron, so hot it was like holding the midday summer sun. I screamed again. My parents, safe in their beds, should have been able to hear me. I had to get rid of this—there was no possible way to hold on to it—and then I saw my cloak. I let go with one arm, grabbed the thick wool, wrapped the iron and half of my right leg in it, and jumped straight into the Mile River.

"The brand fizzled, staining the moon's reflection red. The Mile River winked at me, like a deep, dark eye, and then, standing next to me, wearing nothing at all, was Thom. Looking down on us from the bank was the Fey Queen, her court ranged behind her. She nodded, a very regal gesture, but her voice was as cold as my skin, dressed as it was in river water and night air. 'You are free, my Thom,' she said. 'But beware. Next time'—and here she turned her gaze full on me and me alone—'we will need two.'

"With that vague threat echoing in the night, she smiled, a smile as chill as the night, a smile that never reached her eyes. Then she turned, her hair flowing around her like the river flowing around our calves, and in the time of a blink she and her court were gone.

"I looked at Thom. He was shivering like an aspen leaf in the wind, but he was smiling. In fact, he looked euphoric, and I realized that I must look the same. We caught at each other and clambered out of the river, slipping on the long, frosted grass on the bank, stubbing our toes, and laughing at it all. The simple joy of being well and truly alive.

"'Two, perhaps,' I said, 'but not us. We won't ever let her get us.'

"'No,' Thom said, in a strong voice. 'I swear, whomever she gets, it won't be us or ours.'

"With Thom wrapped in my drenched and torn cloak and me dripping and dragging in my soaked clothes, we stumbled back to Carter House. We shoved through the long grasses and the brambles, worked open the warped front door, built a huge fire, dried off, wrapped ourselves in tattered curtains, and slept the sleep of the victors we were.

"Just before noon the next day, we returned to my family's cottage. After much tea, there was a lengthy reunion between my father and Thom, but it was a reunion with a difference. Thom was no longer just my father's friend. He was young, the same age he'd been those twenty-one years ago. And he was also my love.

"The next day, my father offered Carter House to Thom and me. After one shared look, we declined. Too many ghosts for him, too much house for me. Instead, my parents moved back to my father's boyhood home.

"I would never have believed they would so enjoy restoration work.

"Thom and I? We live in the cottage now. And we raise goats."

❦

When Maisie leaves and returns to the tellers' waiting area, she's met by Maddie and Earl.

"Well done!" cries Maddie.

"An excellent telling," agrees Earl.

"Thank you," says Maisie. "I was worried. Especially about you two." And she sounds so sincere that the elf twins are surprised.

"Did you think we wouldn't approve?" asks Maddie.

"I have to admit, you were the ones I was worried about offending. After all, the Faerie Queen I met wasn't the nicest—well, fey."

"We all have relatives we dislike," Earl says. "Thankfully, we've been lucky enough not to have met her ourselves."

"Ah, but we have heard the stories!" cries Maddie.

"Brrr." Earl pretend shivers.

"Well stated," adds his twin.

❈❈

Magic, Mama Inez reflects. It works in so many ways. Then, from her right side, B.J.'s voice says, "We've been talking about this since we got here." He waves his hand at Wink and Nodia, who are standing a short distance away. "We're sure we've seen you before," and he waits, expectant.

"I do manage to get around," Mama Inez

says with a chuckle in her voice.

B.J. laughs. "Ah. Nicely put. And your dog?"

"Has the most uncanny ability to show up in the strangest places," she says. And she smiles. "And how is your boat?"

"Ha!" B.J. crows. And "Yes. Like I said," he calls to Nodia and Wink. Wink nods wisely, and B.J. reaches out to shake Mama Inez's hand before he goes to tell his story.

The Cabeza River Run

"Most of you will remember that old nursery rhyme about Wynken, Blynken, and Nod."

Nodia, standing at the tent flap, looks up, a quick tilt of her head, then leans over and whispers in Wink's ear. Wink laughs. The rest of the audience waits.

"If this seems like a strange way to start, just keep it in mind while I tell you a story. Legend or coincidence?"

B.J. hears Nodia snort, pretends that he doesn't, and keeps talking.

"On the night in question, our boat is close enough to the Cabeza that we can get her into the water with some judicious pushing and pulling. It's also far enough away that she's not visible to the casual passerby—or floater-by. We want to keep some secrets secret until the River Run. After all, design ingenuity is a big point category.

"The three of us circle the boat, and each looks with a different eye.

"'Bad design' is what Wink says, because he is always, always, the critical eye. I'm stung. I feel a sore spot, just what I would feel if I'd been bee bitten. But this sore spot is in my heart. After all, the *WoSho* is my design. Which, of course, means that I think she's brilliant.

"'Wink, you're doing it again,' Nodia says in the offhand way that shows that she's just barely paying attention to her cranky brother. 'Being negative. Try the positive-thinking thing. B.J.,' she adds without a pause, 'do you think I got your line right here?' Nodia taps the prow. She's the builder, and that's the eye she's using right now.

"'I tried to get the curve in your blueprints, but it was a difficult piece of work.'

"I pretend to look carefully at the area her fingers indicate, but here's the thing. I'm the brains. I do great designs. Really. But then, when I look at the finished product, too much of the time I have trouble matching what I put on paper to what comes out in three dimensions. So I look, and I wrinkle my brow, and I try to act like I'm thinking hard. I can't see a thing that looks wrong, but I'm afraid that Nodia can. I try to figure out what she sees that I might be missing. I try to come up with the exact right thing to say. Next to me, Wink mutters, 'Is it even going to float?'

'Of course she'll float.' Nadia says. She watches Wink with her clear builder's eye as she says, 'She's watertight. Her seams are double sealed. I've triple-checked.'

"Wink walks once around the *WoSho*, all the way around. He stops in front of me and says, 'You knew this question was coming. You knew I'd have to ask. And I hate to live up to your expectations, but there it is. I still have to ask. Why is this boat shaped like a shoe? I was under the impression that we were trying to win the race this year.' He makes the word 'win' sound big and important. And it is. But beauty and imagination have their place as well.

"'I was inspired,' I say. 'I looked at a dog and I saw a boat. Even you have to admit that's a stroke of genius.'

"'I'll admit it's a stroke of something,' Wink says.

"'The curves mimic waves and should slide through the water. The bounce in the sole should take us through that rapids stretch by Sabine's Farm. The raised toe hoists the mast higher than normal to catch even more wind without adding extra length and extra weight.' I beam at him.

"Wink just shakes his head and asks, 'Will we all fit?'

"'Measurements say so,' Nodia says. 'Math never lies.' When Wink looks at her, no expression on his face, she gives in a little and says, 'It's roomier than it looks.'

"'Give it a try,' I urge.

"Wink swings one long leg over the side. For a second he's lopsided, half of him two feet taller than the other half. Then his other leg is up and over and he's standing inside, taking in the view from the boat.

"'Hmpf,' he says after a moment.

"'I was right, wasn't I?' Nodia looks smug.

"Wink doesn't answer, just sits down on one of the bench seats and wiggles his butt into it, getting comfortable.

"'So?' I ask.

"'So—you two climb in with me. Let's try it the way we'll really run the race.'

"I should say here that the Cabeza is a wild river with a bank that moves in and out on itself; a river that's almost schizophrenic in its turns, from calm and flat as a dinner plate to jig-dancing waters. I should also tell you that every year, at the summer solstice, there's a nighttime race down the Cabeza. You may have heard of it. It's quite famous. People come from everywhere.

"But getting down the river in record time, in one piece, with wind, spilled moonlight, and cunning, that's not all. As I said before, there's design ingenuity.

"With the *WoSho*, I thought we'd be grabbing high marks in all categories.

"Nodia and I climb in with Wink. I, being the designer and therefore the captain, take the helm seat. That's when I see that Nodia has carved a good-luck totem inside for all of us. 'Nodia,' I cry, 'it's Eileen!'

"'Yes. The finest cat. And we all know how she loves sailing. I'm sure she'll want to go with us, but she's her own cat, too, and just in case she needs to be somewhere else during the solstice, I thought we should have her with us in spirit.'

"And that, of course, is the exact moment that the long grasses by the Cabeza rustle and there Eileen is, sleek and striped, her eyes reflecting the moon.

"'Come on, then, climb in,' says Wink, and she does, settling down beneath her image as if she's requested this part of the design herself.

"Nodia fiddles a bit with the rudder. Wink, who will navigate, stretches his long legs as if he's still checking the roominess of the *WoSho*, and looks in all directions. I touch the rigging for our sail. Eileen purrs.

"'Comfortable enough?' I ask, and even Wink agrees that the *WoSho* seems to be a very serviceable craft.

"'So,' Nodia finally says. 'Test run?'

"I look to Wink for confirmation. He eyes the nearly full moon. I can almost see the calculations going on in his head. One of the rules of the River Run is: No timepieces. Everything is based on the moon, the connection with the solstice, the twenty-third hour of the longest day of the year. Wink is trying, I know without asking, to make this test as close to the real thing as possible. He answers Nodia's spoken question and my unspoken one. 'Yes,' he says.

"We all get out, except for Eileen, who curls into an even tighter cat ball, and we push. We pull. We correct our course. And finally, we're on the bank of the Cabeza.

"One last shove and the *WoSho* is in the water. She bobs in a contented way, bow curved toward the sky. I squish through the wet river reeds and climb in first. Wink and Nodia follow. A few adjustments with the sail, a flick of the rudder, and we're off.

"The water gleams like rippled silver. The nearly

full moon paints its double in the exact center of the Cabeza. The breeze coming off the water smells of cattails, duckweed, and freesia. I make another slight adjustment to the sail, and it's then that I notice what looks like a tight, smooth patch, sewn with stitches so clean and neat that they look as if they were made by the fey creatures that, in all the handed-down tales told at bedtime, are believed to live in small enclaves up and down the banks of this river.

"'Nodia?' I ask over my shoulder. 'What's this on the sail?'

"Nodia leans slightly. I know because I can feel the *WoSho* respond to the shift in weight. I wiggle my fingers at the place with the stitching, on the lower right side of the sail.

"'Oh. That. I forgot. Mrs. Oldalvi made that.'

"Mrs. Oldalvi. New to town. Long dark hair, red scarves with flashing mirrors, and magic fingers if word of mouth from far away is to be believed.

"'Made the sail, right,' I agree. 'I knew that. But what's this?' My fingers wiggle again.

"'That's what I meant. She put that patch there, too. When I went to pick up the sail, it got caught on a rough spot on her counter. It's such a fine fabric that it tore the smallest bit. She did the patch while I waited. I've seen other sailmakers, haven't you?' This must be a rhetorical question, because she keeps talking without waiting for an answer. 'But she was amazing. I could barely see the thread against the cloth. Can you tell what she stitched?'

"Wink rustles a river chart behind me, and coughs a little cough.

"'Umm. . .' I lean forward and jostle Eileen, who looks at me, her eyes half closed. If a cat could sigh in disgust, that's what she'd be doing. 'Sorry,' I say to her, and I shift both myself and the sail. Then I see it. 'Oh! The evening star.'

"'She knew she was making a River Run sail.'

"'You told her?' Wink asks. He sounds shocked. 'After all our secret planning?'

"Nodia sighs. 'Of course not. She just knew. She said the star patch would give us an edge.'

"I touch it. 'An edge is a good thing.' To the patch I say, 'Work, please.'

"Wink coughs again, and says, 'B.J. I've just found something.'

"'I hope it's something nice.'

"'I suppose that depends on your definition. This year the rapids at Sabine's seem to have spawned a twin.'

"'Is this one of those river jokes?' I ask. 'You know, Knock, knock? Who's there? Rapid. Rapid who? Rapid . . . ?' I sound nervous, I know. Rapids don't sound nice to me. Not at all.

"'No, B.J. And, just as an aside, that sounds like it was shaping up to be a lousy joke.'

"'So 'spawned a twin' means just about what I

think?' I'm still hoping this might turn out to be an example of Wink's often freaky sense of humor.

"'Well, yes.' Wink sounds disgusted, with me or himself I don't know, and also embarrassed. 'There seems to be a brand-new set of rapids about a half mile along. And it looks, on this map, like there may be a whirlpool, too.' He says this like he's saying something that just might be in bad taste in mixed company.

"I turn and look at him, and I'm sure he can see the white all around my eyes. 'Do you think you might have mentioned this a bit earlier?'

"'Well, to be honest,' he says in a quiet voice, 'I didn't really look till now.'

"'I didn't hear that,' I say, and fine, I admit it, I shout, even though I'm convinced now that Wink's disgust and embarrassment are with himself for being lazy, for not doing his homework. I don't bother to tell him that Nodia and I did what we were supposed to do. That even Eileen did her part, by stalking the banks of the Cabeza and looking for dangerous fish. Now Eileen lifts her head again, looks up at me, wary, and sends a nervous look in Wink's direction.

"'Gentlemen!' Nodia shouts. 'We're here. It's there. Let's be proactive and concentrate on getting through. The *WoSho* feels good and solid. She's riding like a champion. We'll be fine. If,' she finishes, 'we concentrate.'

"Eileen meows, a very positive meow, and curls her tail around to her nose. No matter what the situation is, Eileen always agrees with Nodia.

"If Eileen can sleep, if Nodia is confident, everything's got to be under control. I work on getting the feel of the *WoSho* and try not to think about whirlpools. The wind is behind us, the sail catches it, Mrs. Oldalvi's star seems to glow in the light from the overhead moon, and we're moving along at a nice clip.

"All of a sudden I hear voices carried on the breeze. Probably someone else out for a late secret test run. I can't see them, so they can't see us, which is just fine with me. But, as I said, I can hear. Shrieks. Hollers. With a fine-edged sense of panic attached.

"'Whirlpool,' Wink says, and he sounds breathless. I know he's worried.

"I am, too.

"'Better to take a look now than to see it for the first time at solstice.' This is Nodia talking. And she sounds so calm and reasonable that, for the second time in the space of a minute, I let myself relax. 'We'll be judicious,' I say.

"The Cabeza picks up speed. The moon's reflection wavers. Mrs. Oldalvi's evening star glimmers just like the real stars spattered above us and reflected below. The stars, their reflections, and the star on our sail—all look like dancing shards of pure white glass. It's peaceful. It would be much better if I weren't sweating about rapids and whirlpools, but for right here, right now, everything is joining together like a perfectly partnered dance, and I'd be a fool if I couldn't appreciate it.

"Then we round a curve, and there's the ruffle of rapids being pulled into the whirlpool. Whoever was yelping is gone. A good sign. Or a bad one. Either they made it through with no damage, or they were sucked down and are trapped in the river underneath us.

"Wink echoes my thoughts. 'They're gone. That's good. As long as they made it through, of course. Otherwise, they're sleeping with the fishes down below.'

"'Wink!' Nodia screams. 'Stop being so melodramatic. Let's all just concentrate!'

"Eileen is peering over the side. Her moon-reflecting eyes are wide, and for the first time she seems to be doubting this whole adventure.

"'Try cutting it to the left; then, after that series of bouncy ripples, go hard right,' Wink calls.

"And I try. I really do. I can feel Nodia working the rudder like mad. But the *WoSho* has a mind of her own. She heads straight for the whirlpool, on a ninety-degree intercept course.

"We bounce and bump over the first series of waves. The *WoSho* bucks a bit, like a worn-out horse, but she still feels solid. Only the smallest bit of water comes over the sides. Then we're spinning, wide, flat circles that get tighter and sharper as we move closer to the center. And suddenly, just like that, the bouncing and bumping, the twisting and twirling, stop. Everything goes smooth, and I can feel us all breathe out in relief.

"Until, from the back of the boat, I hear Nodia say, 'Uh, B.J. Look down.'

"I do, and when I do, I swallow three or four times, hard. The reason everything has smoothed out is now quite obvious. We've left the Cabeza, and we're airborne.

"'This,' Wink says in a flat voice, 'should not be happening. This should not be possible.' He slaps me on the shoulder, harder than necessary. 'I told you this was a bad design for a boat.'

"'Maybe you should have looked at the map before you got in the boat.'

"'Maybe you should have built something that acted like a boat,' he counters.

"'Maybe,' Nodia calls from the back, 'we've just seen a little of Mrs. Oldalvi's edge. Some of that reputed magic.' And she laughs, a clear, carefree sound.

"Eileen is leaning forward, her neat little front paws on the starboard side of the *WoSho*. She's so far over the edge that I grab and hold tight to the polka-dot bandanna she likes to wear. Edge or not, magic or not, I have to keep my crew together.

"I look up. We're surrounded by ebony-blue sky and cut-glass stars. We're much closer to the moon. I can see the face of the rabbit in the moon that I've heard about, although tonight there's a distinct dog look to that rabbit.

"The night air is cool, and smoother than any water I've ever sailed on.

"I can't help it. I'm grinning in pure happiness when I look back at Wink and Nodia. 'Boat design, edge, magic, whatever. The *WoSho* is making one fantastic airship.'

"Nodia laughs again. She's looking as relaxed as she would be if she were swinging in her hammock. Even Wink is beginning to smile, a slow, lazy smile.

"We dip and curve. The *WoSho* takes care of everything, and our flight seems to go on forever. We can see the Cabeza below us, and the *WoSho* follows its curving course. Then Nodia says, 'We should fly over Sabine's Rapids,' and without any other input, the *WoSho* does a gentle skid to the left.

"'Did you see that?' I yell. 'Did you see that turn? I didn't do a thing! She heard you.'

"Nodia pats the *WoSho* and croons, 'Good boat,' and Wink says, 'Thank you, Mrs. Oldalvi.'

"We see, in the distance, the boat that must have crashed through the whirlpool before us. It looks like the whirlpool took a bite out of it. It's listing to port. But we're just fine. We act like little kids. We reach up and try to touch Orion's belt. We wave at the Seven Sisters. We call to the rabbit-dog in the moon, and act as if he's going to answer. We issue commands, and the *WoSho* responds like we've been working together for years. The tiny star on our sail glows with the same clean moonlight as the stars above us.

"Our flight seems to go on forever. But even something magically good has to come to an end. Of her own accord, the *WoSho* comes down, close to where the finish line for the River Run will be in less than twenty-four hours. She settles back on the Cabeza with the barest of ripples, and a tiny splosh.

"Wink, Nodia, Eileen, and I sit quietly in our resting ship. The *WoSho* bobs on the water as if she's dancing a slow waltz. Peace and contentment spread over us like a favorite quilt.

"'Well,' Nodia finally says, which could mean any-thing.

"'Yeah,' Wink agrees. 'Absolutely.'

"Eileen purrs and pats her totem.

"I laugh, feeling a little giddy. 'Not such a bad design after all.'

"'With a thank-you to Mrs. Oldalvi,' Nodia says, echoing her brother.

"'Yep. Even without my design, that would have been quite an edge.' I'm still smiling.

"After several minutes of rocking on the Cabeza, Wink says, in a dreamy sort of voice, 'I'm not putting a lot of effort into this, but I am kind of wondering. Maybe you are, too. How do we get back to where we started?'

"'Huh.' He's got me, because I haven't been won-dering about this at all. But it's a valid point. At the end of the River Run, they always tugboat everyone back to wherever, so this is a problem none of us ever mentioned when we were having those long, tedious talks about test runs. I finally decide to just ask the *WoSho*: 'Can you take us home? Back up the river?' And I pat her side, just like Nodia did, just like I would pat Eileen if she were sitting on my lap.

"The *WoSho* turns around, obedient as a well-trained puppy, levitates just the slightest bit above the Cabeza, and glides back home.

"We clamber out, one by one, and because we're in the water again, I pass Eileen to Wink, who then passes her to Nodia. When Eileen is safely on shore, we push and drag the *WoSho* back into her hiding place.

"I check the boat from all angles, to make sure she's hidden, and I pat her one more time. 'We'll keep you forever,' I whisper.

"Nodia rubs the prow, rubs it as she would a magic lantern. In some way, that's just what the *WoSho* is. The magic part, anyway.

"Wink nods once. 'We'll see you tomorrow night,'

he says, and it's clear that he's attached himself to the *WoSho* as much as Nodia and I have.

"But 'Will we?' Nodia asks. 'I mean, should we? It was wonderful. Fantastic. But if we fly tomorrow night, won't we be disqualified?'

"Wink looks at the *WoSho*, a thoughtful expression on his face. Then he shrugs and says, 'We'll just tell her not to do anything tricky. It'll be fine.' And he starts walking through the reeds toward the road that leads back to town.

"Nodia laughs and says, 'For someone who's usually so negative, you're coming across as pretty sure of yourself.'

"Wink glances over his shoulder. 'Yep.' And he nods his head. 'It'll be fine.'

"'The rapids?' asks Nodia.

"Wink shrugs again. 'No problem. We'll just tell her.' He grins at his sister. 'I've got all the confidence in the world in her.'

"Before Nodia can say anything else, I catch up with them. I've been thinking about something that doesn't have a thing to do with rapids, or with tomorrow night. I clear my throat. 'I'm sort of hesitant about saying this, but is anyone else thinking about that old bedtime story?'

"'Hmm?' That's Nodia, a half smile on her face, still watching her brother.

"'I know it sounds silly, but Wink and Nodia? Like Wynken and Nod? And B.J. could be Blynken? And a flying boat that looks like a shoe? Doesn't it all just seem kind of familiar?'

"Nodia transfers her attention to me. She wrinkles her nose. 'Oh, I don't know. That's just a nursery rhyme. I don't think those things are based on anything but meter and rhythm and a cute little story to get kids to sleep. You didn't think about it when you designed the boat, did you?'

"I shake my head no.

"'Right. I think we can just thank Mrs. Oldalvi and her sail.' She glances at Wink. 'Magic, right?'

"'Why not?' he says.

"As for me? Magic, of course. But the idea for the kind of magic?

"'Nodia,' I say, 'did you happen to talk about the *WoSho*'s design with Mrs. Oldalvi?'

"'Well, yes, a bit. We wanted to make sure the sail was the exact right size and shape.'

"'Ha,' I say, triumphant. 'I knew she had to fine-tune that magic to something. All this stuff, it's got to start somewhere. I might not have made the connection when I designed the *WoSho*, but I'll bet she did.'

"Nodia frowns, the little line above her nose showing in the moonlight. 'But B.J., I'm sure she didn't tear the sail on purpose. In fact, I think I was taking it from her when it tore. And if that hadn't happened, she wouldn't have had to patch it. So . . .' She trails off, but she doesn't have to go any further.

"'Nursery rhyme, B.J.,' says Wink very firmly. 'You said it first. We never thought about our names in that context before. And we didn't think about it when we looked at the WoSho. Why would Mrs. Oldalvi get there?'

"'Because,' I say, more to myself than to them, 'she's got magic in her fingertips.'

"But Wink shakes his head and says, 'I think coincidence is all we've got here.'"

❦❦

"The next night, twenty-one and a half hours into the longest day, we're at the starting line for the River Run with the WoSho. There are boats all around us, but there's nothing that looks anything like ours. I can hear snickers from all sides. I ignore them, and Wink, Nodia, and Eileen do the same. I pat the WoSho for luck and settle my crew inside. When Eileen snugs in under her totem, I see that she's wearing a yellow bandanna instead of her usual polka-dot one. Yellow for luck.

"The whole town is either racing or on the banks, watching. I see Mrs. Oldalvi. Her expression is serene. Nodia waves to her, and she raises her hand, palm facing us, and smiles.

"'Ready?' I ask.

"Wink stares at the shifting sky. There are clouds tonight. The rabbit-dog moon is hiding. But Wink knows when to start anyway, and he says, 'Anytime, B.J.'

"Nodia shifts in her seat. 'Are you sure? Remember, we need to be at the finish right at the end of the twenty-third hour.'

"'Nodia. I know,' he says. 'I'm not an amateur.' And Eileen meows.

"'Gone, then,' I say. 'Eileen and Wink agree. One, two, three, and we're on our way. Mrs. Oldalvi waves once more, and the Cabeza takes us.

"The river is fast tonight. Choppy. All winds seem to be crosswinds. I make constant sail corrections, and

Nodia flicks the rudder around, her wrist moving like a hummingbird flitting from flower to flower.

"'Sabine's coming up!' Wink calls. Eileen curls into an extra-tight ball. From around the bend I hear other boats creak and groan, other riders cry and curse.

"I breathe in and yell, 'Hang on!' I glance over my shoulder and see both Wink and Nodia, eyes wide. They're staring straight ahead. Nodia cries, 'B.J.!'

"I whip around just in time to see the Cabeza standing up on its hind legs in a black wave taller than the *WoSho*. We're surrounded by blackness, water, sky.

"'Sabine's!' Wink yells. 'Remember the whirlpool!' And then it happens. Without any of us saying another word, the *WoSho* does a little two-step and we're up and out of there.

"Tonight the sky is different. There are no stars to guide us, no moon to shine on our sail. Just wind and black and now, far to the south, lightning flashes. Below, the Cabeza is the blackest thing in our black world, but I see lights near Sabine's and what looks like a welter of broken boats.

"We fly over the whirlpool and the rapids. The lightning flashes closer. Too close. It seems to singe the air. Wink yells, 'Down! Now!' and the *WoSho* lowers her nose and goes into a gentle glide toward the river.

"We touch down right before the finish line. Just ahead of us is a fast little kayak, polished gold-green fiberglass gleaming in the lights from the festival held in conjunction with the River Run. The kayak skips across the finish line to a burst of applause. We follow, and we all know we're too late. 'And we flew,' Nodia says, sounding wistful. 'Even with design points, I don't think there's any way we can take first.' The rest of us are quiet.

"I move the sail and we tack to the bank. Mrs. Oldalvi is right there, as if she's been waiting for us. She doesn't say a word, just looks at us with her eyebrows raised. I know Nodia sees her because suddenly she laughs, and Mrs. Oldavi laughs along with her.

"'Wink says, 'That was the best ride of my life. Even better than last night. The wind . . .'

"'. . . and the lightning!' Nodia adds.

"'The waves!'

"'The black!'

"I listen to them exchange exclamations. I don't join in. I just pat my boat and grin at Mrs. Oldalvi. 'Who cares about winning?' I say. 'We've got magic.'"

"Thanks to Mrs. Oldalvi," B.J. says as he passes Mama Inez. She laughs, raises her hand palm out, and they tap fingers. Toby rubs against B.J.'s leg. B.J. looks down and studies Toby's face. Then he adds, "And to that rabbit-dog in the moon."

The only man left in the waiting area who hasn't shared his story comes up to B.J. "I've got to say I'm on your side. I think there's something going on with your story and that little rhyme. In fact, after everything I've heard tonight, I have the feeling that my story puts me square in the middle of normal. Flying boats, giant beanstalks, legs that turn into fins, lizard men, the fey." He shakes his head. "I think what I have to say is going to sound quite tame."

"Shall we see what they think?" Mama Inez asks, gesturing toward the audience.

Zola thinks of Tris, and the thought makes him relax. It's almost as if Tris were here with him, giving him a boost of energy strong as his morning cup of coffee. He takes a long, deep breath, says, "Absolutely," and walks with even strides to the front of the tent.

Mattresses

"IT'S NOT EASY BEING a prince. I know, I know. It looks glamorous. And the glitter and glitz are enough to make anyone who hasn't grown up surrounded by the opulence stand with mouth agape. But when you've been around it long enough, one golden chandelier begins to look too much like the next; one tapestry of elk hunts fades into another of maidens dancing in the spring. And no matter how many fires burn in the rooms in winter, it's always abysmal, and cold. Cold, and damp as the lake when the ice is too thin and a careless step can cause a soaking that can lead to a freezing and possible hypothermia.

"And then, of course, there's the maintenance of the family line. That creaky old conundrum. Example: My mother, always the diplomat, would say, 'Zola'——

that's me—'there's a lovely young thing over in the next duchy.' Then she'd wink at me and add, 'Wide hips. Excellent childbearing possibilities.'

"I would sigh loudly, to show that I wasn't at all interested in either childbearing possibilities or wide hips. My father would hear and pick up on my reluctance. 'You do plan on keeping this kingdom together, don't you, my boy?' He'd pretend to be jovial. In reality, he was making a threat.

"The three of us would then sit and look at one another, all wary for different reasons.

"It was actually quite amazing that we carried on discussions at all. None of us ever seemed to be talking about the same thing, whether it was what was on the dinner menu, my prospects for snaring a bride, or anything in between.

"'Snaring.' Nice word, don't you think? Because that's exactly what they were doing, those parents of mine. They were setting a trap. They hadn't quite got to the pointed stakes at the bottom of the pit, but believe me, they were very close. They'd been throwing princesses, and duchesses, and whatever other nobility they could lay their hands on, at me ever since I'd made that swing, twist, and drop into puberty. It was as if we were involved in some never-ending game of catch-the-ball, and I was the one who kept dropping the damned thing. Quite on purpose, I assure you. And I always had excellent reasons. Too short. Too old. Too fat. Too tall. Can't ride. Rides too well. Can't cook. Can't speak. Too— Oh, you get the idea.

"My royal parents were beginning to get annoyed. Which says quite a bit about both their patience and my persistence.

"They're good people, my parents. They just didn't have even the smallest clue about who and what I was. I, you see, was looking for a prince.

"'Zola, I have an excellent idea!' My mother was crowing, she was so pleased with her new scheme. I should explain at this point that schemes were, and still are, my mother's forte.

"'Enough of these too-much or not-enough excuses, my boy.' This was my father, still making an effort to sound cheerful, but I knew my father, and I knew that what he really was, was angry. As his only heir, I'd been thwarting his plans for handing over a perfectly good kingdom for way too many years. He had had enough, which is perhaps why he was going along with this latest scheme of my mother's, which would, in her true fashion, prove to be completely scatterbrained.

"The scheme was as follows.

"My mother was saying, '. . . multiple mattresses, one on top of the other. Say four. Or seven. Something like that. It will probably depend on thicknesses. Or space. Or the height of that ladder we found in . . .'.

"My father cleared his throat. 'Melicant, my dear. You're doing it again. Tangenting.'

"One of her favorite pastimes, second only to

scheming. She did it so often, we'd even made it a verb in our household lexicon.

"'Oh. My. So sorry.' She gave us a sheepish smile. 'Now, where was I?'

"This was the next usual step. Confusion, followed by a turn back on track, usually with a nudge from my father or me.

"'Mattresses,' said my father, who was beginning to look tired, beginning to look as if he thought this was a bad idea after all.

"Now she beamed. 'Of course. Mattresses. With a pea at the bottom. Underneath all five, or eight. Or nine. It depends, of course . . .'

"'Melicant.' My father sounded desperate.

"'Yes, dear. And whoever feels the pea, she'll be the one. A true sensitive noble, ready for you to marry. No excuses.'

"I moaned. Loudly.

"My father glared. Arrow eyes.

"My mother kept smiling. Sunshine through the clouds. Everything will be all right.

"I felt like I was six.

"I debated inwardly. Tell them, don't tell them? Which way to go? I loved them, and I knew just how hard they were trying, knew just how much an heir meant to them. And I had absolutely no idea of what to say, or of how to say it.

"So I sat there, and they took my lack of objection for acquiescence, and the parade began.

"I assure you, it was a parade. Just like the beginning of the circus, when all the possibilities were waiting, glowing with promise. Where anything could happen, and probably would. Unfortunately, in reality those glowing promises all proved to be shams.

"The noble ladies started coming—in droves. From what I could see, as I kept out of sight and watched from my tower windows, they were all Too. Too of everything. Or nothing. Our castle began to feel like an inn with an ever-changing cast of guests.

"Tempers began to flare. The laundress, hanging out basket upon basket of sheets to flap in the cool autumn breezes, looked ready to pack her bag. Anytime I ventured near the kitchens, I heard the cook banging pots much more than ever before and swearing loudly. This at least was useful, as I discovered a few handy words I hadn't yet learned. The stableboys were beside themselves with the work of keeping our stalls in a constant state of readiness.

"My parents? My father began to look exhausted. My mother's smile began to fray around the edges.

"I became quite snappish.

"And still the ladies came. I watched them come. I watched them go. None of them looked any worse for the test night atop the pile of mattresses. None of them looked, in the morning, like a sensitive noble who has spent a restless night because of a lump in her bed.

"In the morning, none of their appetites seemed at all affected.

"My mother was becoming distraught. My father was becoming depressed. I was simply worn out. I had, in fact, after a fortnight of this travesty, made up my mind. I would tell them. How could having a son who was gay be any more wearing than having a parade of useless noble ladies tramping through their house? Ladies who were coming for just one thing—the chance to lock themselves to my father's kingdom.

"I'd finally decided that that night, at the evening meal, I would simply tell them.

"Then, that afternoon, the storm blew in. Our castle, as usual for a well-fortified place of residence, sat atop a hill. This meant that from my tower, on all sides, I could see storms before anyone else was willing to believe we were soon going to be drenched.

"I loved to watch the wild, free spirit of furiously strong weather. I reveled in the flashes of lightning, the whipping of tree branches, the churning mix of gray and white clouds. I'd watched storms from my tower for as long as I could remember.

"But I've never seen a storm like that one, before or since.

"Trees weren't just whipping, they were bending at ninety-degree angles. Clouds weren't just churning, they were being thrown at one another with the force of rocks pitched from a catapult. At one point all the clouds meshed into the face of a woman with long, wind-whipped hair. I saw her turn and look straight at me, I swear. And the lightning? From all sides, at all times. My tower felt as if it were caught on the edge of a tornado, as if it were being twisted in seven different directions at once.

"I am not ashamed to admit that I was crouching on the floor, my eyes at windowsill level. I was both terrified and awed by what was happening around me. Then, through sheets of rain the color of brick mortar and with the opacity of oily smoke, I saw a rider approaching from the north. Rider and horse were losing two meters of ground for every three that they gained, but slowly, so slowly, they made their way to the castle drawbridge.

"Once they crossed that bridge, I applauded. What a show of bravery, fortitude, constancy. Or, more likely, a desire to get inside—inside anywhere away from that weather.

"It mattered very little which it was. I still had a great desire to meet him. Or her.

"By the time I made it down the stairs, he (for it was a he, and even wet and bedraggled, a rather attractive he at that) was standing on the rushes in the great hall. Water poured off him in rivers, and even in the relatively dry (there are always leaks in a castle) and somewhat warm room, he was shivering. He barely looked at me. All his attention was focused on my father, who was saying, '. . . stay the night. Your horse is being cared for?' My father. He would ask that.

"The dripping stranger nodded and said, 'My thanks.' He looked ready to topple sideways and to sleep where he landed. This my father noticed, at the same time that he noticed me. 'Zola, take him up to that noble lady'— sarcasm here, please note—'room. At least we know there's a bed there that's usable. I doubt we'll have any princesses or duchesses wanting to use it tonight.'

"'Of course.'

"But before I could lead the stranger away, my father added, 'Your name, sir?'

"He pulled in breath, visibly drawing on his remaining strength to answer my father's question. 'Dragoran, sir. Tris Dragoran.'

"Tris. A shortened version of Tristan, perhaps? A knight's name?

"I wanted to ask, wanted to know much more. But as I led Tris up the stairs, he began to sway. I grabbed him to keep him upright, and the next thing I knew, my arm was around him and I was half dragging him along. He smelled of rain, wet hair, horse, and the acrid kind of sweat that starts up when you begin to fear for your life.

"By the time I had him in what my father had referred to as the noble lady room, he was barely with me. The climbing drag up the stairs seemed to have used whatever reserves of strength he might have had left. He was a dead weight against me, and enough rain had transferred between us that I was almost as wet and bedraggled as he.

"'Here we are,' I said, trying to sound bouncy. Tris dragged his eyes open wider than the slits they'd been while we'd careened down the hall. I could almost feel the muscles in his eyelids gather to do their work. And then he saw the ladder that reached to the top of the eight or twelve mattresses.

"'Oh, please,' he moaned. 'I have to climb?'

"'Well,' I said after a moment. 'I could prop you

up in the corner and take a few of those away. Get it down to five or seven.'

"'No.' Then, as if realizing how brusque he'd sounded, he said, 'If you could stay a moment and help . . . I think me climbing once rather than waiting for you to climb multiple times is all I can manage. Do you mind?'

"I shook my head, quite taken with his look of determination and his golden lion's eyes.

"It was a struggle, but we made it. Tris seemed to fall asleep the minute he hit the top mattress. I pulled a cover over him, hoping it would help absorb the rain, climbed down the ladder, and left.

"It was only then, looking through the open door of the great hall from the staircase, that I saw that the storm had passed. The sun was out, steam rose from the ground like boil from a kettle, and all the clouds were gone but one. And that one cloud looked exactly like the cloud woman from the storm. She faced me once again, but now there was a gentle smile on her face. Then the winds shifted, the cloud disappeared, and all that was left was the washed blue sky.

"Tris did not join us at the evening meal. Which gave my mother, my father, and me all the opportunity we needed to speculate.

"'It's a fine horse, that one he rode up on,' my father said.

"'Fought that storm like a demon,' I said. 'I watched from my tower.'

"'Poor things,' my mother said, and her sympathy was obviously for both Tris and his horse. 'How far do you suppose they came?'

"'Don't know any Dragorans,' my father said. 'But it's rich leather on that horse.'

"'And fine enough clothes on him, too,' I pointed out.

"My mother tapped her index finger against her jaw. 'Interesting,' she said."

"Two in the morning, with milk-white moonlight pouring through my tower window and spilling across my pillow like liquid from a broken jug. I couldn't sleep, no matter how much I twisted and turned.

"You'd have thought my mother had put peas under my mattress, hundreds of them, several centimeters deep.

"I decided to see if Tris was awake, perhaps hungry after all that riding and no dinner. I knocked gently on his door.

"'Come in!' he called, and his voice sounded harried.

"Come in I did, and I saw him wrestling with that tower of mattresses. I started to ask what he was up to when it hit me with all the force of the winds from the day before. I wanted to be sure, though, so I was quite cautious when I said, 'Trouble sleeping?'

"He looked at me, and the look was equal parts of disgust and chagrin. 'Sorry.' He shoved at another mattress and looked at the piles cluttering the floor. 'Very sorry. About the mess, about the noise. I didn't mean to wake you.'

"I shook my head and stepped onto and then over a small pile of three mattresses. 'Didn't wake me at all. What's wrong?' And silly as it sounds, I mentally crossed my fingers. Please, I thought, say there's something under the mattresses. Please.

"'I think,' Tris said, 'there's something under the mattresses. I thought I'd just move them, get it out, and that would be that.' He looked again at the mess. 'It seems to be more trouble than I expected.'

"I wanted to grab him and hug him, or jump up and down in glee, but I stayed calm and said, 'Let's just check all the way down to the bottom. After all, you only have two or five left.'

"Together we tossed the rest of the mattresses aside. And there, as I'd known it would be, was a dried golden pea.

"I picked it up. 'The culprit,' I said.

"'That?' Tris's voice went up a few notches. 'Please. It couldn't be that.'

"I thought about how to explain this, then started with 'That mother of mine . . .'

❧

"Tris joined us for breakfast, but he picked at his food, and he looked somewhat worse for the wear of his sleepless night. It had been closing in on four when I'd finished explaining my mother's plot, and we'd spent some time talking about other things as well. His lion eyes, my raven locks, and—well, really, that's all you need to know.

"What we hadn't talked about was how to break things to my parents.

"Finally, in an effort to get him to say something,

anything, at the breakfast table, I asked how he'd slept.

"He looked surprised. 'You don't remember?'

"'Umm—tell them?' I suggested, pointing at my mother and my father, who, after my question, were watching me warily.

"Tris shrugged, then said, 'Not well, I'm afraid. I don't mean to sound ungrateful, but I was up much of the night. Zola came to check on me in the early morning, and between us, we found the problem.' He held the golden pea out for their inspection. 'Once we'd moved this, things improved considerably.'

"'Zola!' my mother cried.

"'I never told,' I swore. 'Tell her, Tris. Tell her I didn't say a thing until you'd told me about that sharp, pointy thing digging into your back.'

"'True,' Tris said. 'I promise, I'm not usually so sensitive. Roget, my horse, and I have spent many nights in unusual and uncomfortable places. And when I saw my problem was a small pea . . .' His voice trailed off. And he blushed. Endearing. And attractive as hell.

"There was a silence that almost rang around our table. My mother finally said, 'Does this mean what I think it means?'

"My father said, 'No wonder none of those women were interesting to you.'

"I sighed, a sigh of pure relief.

"Perhaps you've already guessed the end. Nothing is ever easy, though, so there was shouting, explaining, hand wringing; crying, laughing, and sheer giddiness. But my parents are my parents, and eventually they accepted what I'd known and they'd suspected for a long time. I was a gay prince. And I felt that I'd finally met my other half.

"But Tris, even after all that early-morning talking, had never given me an unequivocal yes. So I had to ask, even though my parents were still sitting side by side at the table. 'Are you sure? Do you really want to do this?'

"Tris looked directly at me, wrinkled his brow as if he couldn't understand how I could be confused, and said, 'Well, Zola, of course.' There was no hesitation at all.

"My union with Tris has united my kingdom and the far northern duchy of Dragoran. It appears that heirs will not be forthcoming. Of course, one never knows. It appears that my mother is working on this scheme . . ."

❧❧

The audience is smiling and laughing as Zola leaves. He is quite pleased, and he can't wait to get home and tell Tris how it all went. Tris, he knows, will especially enjoy the laughter, one of the things they do best together. As he returns to the tellers' waiting area, he sees that Mama Inez is laughing, too.

"In the middle of normal," she says. "After that story?"

"Of course," he says. Then, as an afterthought, he adds, "Everything except for the storm. That was quite impressive."

"As if it had been meant to be," Mama Inez agrees, and she watches for his reaction.

Zola looks at her long and hard, then laughs himself. "It was you, wasn't it? That bundle of clouds. It had to be."

Mama Inez shrugs her right shoulder, a casual movement. "Magic," she says.

"Magic," Zola repeats, still smiling. "And all this time I was just going with a happy coincidence. Wait until I tell Tris."

As Zola walks through the waiting area, he passes the two who still wait to go out to the teller's cushion. One of them is Sue, Lightning's friend and rider. She says, "No magic like that in my story. Maybe some events people'd see as overblown, things I think they might find interesting, but nothing even close to magic."

Zola stops. "You never know. Look at me. Proof positive. I never even thought about magic."

"Sometimes, when you're in the middle of it, you don't recognize it," agrees Rosey, who's the last teller of the evening.

Mama Inez comes up behind Zola, her eyes shining. She seems to be glowing from the inside out. "Ready?" she asks Sue.

Sue swallows, hard. "I was, until about two seconds ago," she says in a whisper. Then she looks at Mama Inez, and looks again. "Do you have a sister? You look so much like someone who used to live in—"

She's interrupted by Zola, who throws his arm around her shoulders. "You'll be fine out there."

He points to the waiting audience. "They're ready to hear anything, to support anything. Best of all, they're willing to believe anything."

"Easy for you. You're a prince and all." Sue sighs, forgetting about Mama Inez and her possible sister.

Sue reaches over and pats Lightning, who looks at her, his liquid brown eyes steady and sharp.

The Lizard Man, who seems to have adopted Lightning as his own, says, "I am not a prince. I told my story."

Lightning simply whinnies.

Sue says, "Hmpf." Then she puts one foot in front of the other and mumbles, "The only thing to fear is fear its own self."

The Colors of Lightning

"I DO LOVE TO ride, and that's what I was doing the first time that handsome Pecos Bill saw me. And, for that matter, the first time I saw him. I was riding the biggest catfish in the county. Only saw him for a minute, though, catfish being what they are, and this one in particular bucking and bouncing like a bronc who's positively against the idea of being broke.

"That fish and me was under the water again before I could holler out so much as a 'Good day,' but even in that short a time I could see that Bill, riding some gorgeous stallion for all he was worth, was one to be reckoned with.

"Now, you might be asking yourself, 'What is it with that Slewfoot Sue? Why is she a-riding on a catfish, for Lord's sake?'

"All I can tell you is it's a sight better than riding a broom around a kitchen and picking up after a man. And I have always loved a challenge.

"I saw him for the second time at the county picnic on Independence Day. There was everything there, just like you'd expect. Corn on the cob, sweet melons, beans dripping with molasses, slabs of barbecue, hunks of cornbread soaking up honey, and chilies so hot, felt like the roof of your mouth was blown right off. Whiskey and pure spring-water beer. Three-legged races for the little ones. And, late that night, fireworks shooting colors out to the moon.

"It was after one of the big sunburst fireworks exploded, the kind that look like the whole world's caught on fire, that I saw Bill again. This time he weren't riding his horse. No sir. This time he was hanging on to one of them tails of that starburst firework, sailing acrost the sky, headed for who knew where. Looked like that man liked a challenge as much as me.

"That was when I knew I had to meet him. But as luck would have it, when he came down from that firework tail, he landed over to Bexar County, up north, and he weren't able to get back down to home until a good bit later.

"So I took that time while he was gone to start asking around. Talked to some who knew some who knew of him. Talked to some who knew some who knew him. Finally talked to some who knew him theirselves. And found out then that he'd been asking around about me.

"Maeve Maginty, down to the general store, she said, 'He saw you riding that big rainbow catfish lives over in the river, down to the aqueduct, Sue. Says you were quite a sight.' Maeve winked. 'Seems smitten, girl.'

"I sniffed, my nose in the air. 'He can seem smitten, Maeve, all he wants. I'd rather be riding that old catfish any day than taking care of some man.' Which was generally true, but truth be told, I was feeling the bittiest bit smitten myself. I weren't ready to be tied down, no sir. But if I'd been asked, I'd've had to admit that I found Bill occupying a good piece of my mind.

"I wanted to keep Maeve off track, though, so I added, 'He does have one fine horse. Like to take a ride on that one, I would.'

"Maeve Maginty laughed so hard, she had to hang on to her selling counter to keep from falling down onto the floor and dirtying her dress on the sawdust.

"'Ride Lightning? Why, girl, you got as much chance of doing that as you do of getting that forever bachelor Bill to settle down in amongst the piney woods and raise a passelful of kids!'

"I sniffed again, much louder, stood tall as I was able, and said, 'Maeve, I weren't talking about riding him. I was talking about riding his horse.'

"Which made Maeve Maginty stop laughing and

start to blushing mighty fast, and gave me a chance to make my escape.

"So now, not only was I thinking that Bill was a kind of fine-looking man, I was also half crazy to ride this horse that Maeve Maginty thought I couldn't ride. I mean, my mama didn't raise no fool, and I was pretty sure of what I could and could not do. I didn't put on airs and say I could do things I couldn't, and I wouldn't take no bets on something I thought was foolish, not ever. But that horse Lightning—I was just real sure that he and I could come to an understanding, same as me and that old catfish. And I aimed to find Bill and prove that the feeling in my gut was right. Maybe, in fact, both the feeling in my gut as well as the one that was starting to tickle my heart, too.

"I guess Maeve must've told Bill about me showing an interest in that horse of his, because the next thing I knowed, who was knocking at my door but the man himself?

"'Howdy,' I says, sounding cool as the springhouse on a hot day in August. But I gotta tell you true, inside me, my heart was tippy-tapping fit to beat the band. That man was real handsome up close. And he was holding his hat in his hand, exactly like a gentleman come to call.

"'Right pleased to meet you, ma'am.' He smiled, and I thought I'd done died and gone to heaven. Them blue eyes, with little laugh crinkles. 'I hear you've been talking around town about my Lightning.'

"'That I have,' I agreed. 'Sure would like to ride a fine-looking horse like that.'

"Bill, he just laughed. It were a good laugh, strong and sure. But I do not like being laughed at, no sir.

"I straightened up tall, just like I done in Maeve Maginty's store, and said, 'Never seen a horse I couldn't ride.'

"Bill, he just nodded and said, real polite, 'Ma'am, I believe you have now. Lightning don't let nobody ride him but me. It's just,' he added, almost an apology, 'this understanding we've got worked out.'

"I could see Lightning now. He was tied to the low branch of the apple tree, down close to the road. He'd been hid by the barn till now, so he must've been moving around, cropping my good grasses and no doubt munching on wind-falled apples. I watched him through eyes that were half shut against the sun.

"'Bet he and I could come to an understanding, too.'

"Bill, he turned his back to me, and ladies, you'll understand when I say he looked as good in back as he did in front. He eyed his horse, and Lightning, as if he knowed he was being seen, swished his tail in the sun till it glowed bright as the North Star on a no-moon night. When Bill turned back to me, there was this speculating look in his eyes.

"'That was you rode that big old rainbow catfish down to the creek, weren't it?'

"I allowed as how yes, that'd been me.

"'It was bucking pretty good,' he said. 'I remember. In and out of that water, up and down like a double stripe of rainbow, looking for the sun.'

"I agreed, then added, 'Sometime, riding something like that, you got to use real good breath control. Got to be pretty calm. Got to have some faith.'

"Bill nodded, as if to say, 'I reckon you do need all them things,' turned to look at Lightning again, then to look back to me.

"'We might could give it a try,' he said at last. He spoke real slow, dragging them words out almost to tomorrow.

"'I'll just get my boots.' I was gone and back before he could change his mind.

"Me and Bill walked out to Lightning, not saying one word. Just before we got to the horse, Bill said, 'Wait here for just a minute. Him and me, we got to talk.'

"I stayed put. A whole lot of whispering and whick-ering went on, and then Bill said to me, 'Well, you got a bitty chance. But I will say he is not real pleased.'

"'It'll be just fine,' I said, but now, right up next to Lightning, I was feeling that nervous. One, he was a big horse, bigger'n I'd thought. And a sight bigger'n that old catfish. Two, I was all of a sudden not wanting to look stupid in front of Bill. Just in case this didn't work out quite the way I had things planned.

"But if my mama didn't raise no fool, she didn't raise no coward, neither, and she was always preach-ing, 'The only thing to fear is fear its own self.' So I took a deep breath, held out my hand for Lightning to nudge at, then settled my boot in the left stirrup and swung my leg up and over.

"We walked two steps together, Lightning and me, and then he seen Bill standing off to his left. Which must have been about the time he realized that I was the one on his back. He took one startled look over his shoulder, then bucked his back feet so high, there was no way in tarnation that I could have held on. I was up and out of that saddle afore I could blink.

"Remember when I told you Bill took that fireworks tail up north? Well, now I was seeing what he must have seen on his trip. I was so high in the sky, I went right on through the middle of the afternoon clouds gathering to make us some well-needed rain, skinned on out the top, and thought I'd burn my flailing fingertips on the sun.

"And then I started down, straight on down, gravity pulling at me the whole way. When I bottomed out of them clouds, I could see Bill and Lightning both looking up, seeming real interested in what was happening to me. Then Bill reached up and took his rope off Lightning's saddle horn, done something fancy with some knots, looked at me again, and swung. That lasso sailed up like it had a life of its own, sailed right past me, and then settled around my shoulders, neat as a wedding veil floats over a bride.

"Next thing I knowed, I was being gentled back to earth, brought down like a favorite quilt being took off the laundry line on a quiet Sunday.

"I landed, and my feet did a quick-step version of the Cotton-Eyed Joe to help keep me upright. I had just about caught my breath when Bill come up to me, coiling his rope, and said, 'Ma'am, that were the bravest thing I ever did see. Will you marry me?'

"I looked into them blue eyes with the laugh crinkles, and I done thought a long time, long enough that Bill fidgeted some and Lightning whickered at me. I was wanting to say yes, but I didn't never plan on being tied to any man. So I said, 'Thank you, Bill, but I got to think on that.'

"Bill, he said, 'Hmm,' Lightning snorted a horse snort, and away they went.

"I thought that was that and I never'd see either of them again. But the next morning, bright and early, who should be knocking on my front door but Bill? He stood on my porch, all gentlemanly. His hat was in one hand, and in his other was a basket of the biggest, reddest strawberries I ever done seen.

"'Little present for you, ma'am,' he said, sounding kinda bashful.

"What could I do? I invited him in, made him coffee, sliced up some bread, and sat down to breakfast. Lightning watched us through the window. After we was done eating, Bill said, 'Ma'am, will you marry me?'

"But there was something held me back, and all I could say was 'Thank you, Bill, but I got to think on that.'

"Next afternoon, up to my house comes Isabelle Swann, the town's brand-new postmistress. My place was starting to look like a watering hole in the middle of the prairie, with all these visitors. Isabelle was carrying this big book, and soon as I seen it, I knew it was the brand-new Wishing Book. If you ain't seen one, let me tell you, there's everything in there from stoves to dishes, from tools to dresses.

"Isabelle, she and I had talked a little and she knowed I was looking for a posthole digger so I could fix that falling-down fence around the corral, so she'd brought that Wishing Book right out. We was sitting on the porch, drinking cold tea, when she opened the book to a page of white, white wedding dresses.

"'Must have marked the wrong page,' she said. 'These aren't posthole diggers.' Her red scarf fluttered in the hot breeze. The mirrors on the scarf flashed in the sun. 'Huh. Oh well, this one's pretty, don't you think, Sue?' Her finger and that scarf both tapped a picture of a light, lacy-looking thing, long and bouncy with hoops and a bustle.

"I got to tell you, I've always thought both hoop-skirts and bustles was the most useless things ever. And I got to admit, I still thought so. But there was something about that dress, yes sir, and damn if all of a sudden didn't I want both a useless bustle and a useless hoopskirt! I sighed, 'Oh, that is downright lovely.'

"Two days later, at dusk time when you can just start to count fireflies, Bill showed up at my house again. This time he was carrying a bunch of bluebonnets, the same color blue as his eyes. I invited him to sit a spell while I put them flowers in some water. When I come back, Bill says, 'Ma'am, will you marry me?' and Lightning, he whickered and dropped his muzzle over the porch rail.

"I thought on the strawberries and the bluebonnets. I thought on trying to ride Lightning and Bill saving me. I thought on Isabelle and the Wishing Book. And I thought, Third time's the charm, just like in the fairy stories.

"What could I say but yes? 'But there is one thing I need to do before I can marry you, Bill.'

"'And what would that be?'

"'Get me that storybook wedding dress I done saw in the Wishing Book.'

"Bill allowed as to how he guessed he could wait a bit, and I hurried into the house to grab my mail-order book. Now, you order some things from the Wishing Book and it does take an amount of time to get to you. And, tell you true, the wait for that dress was a good thing. Gave me and Bill some few weeks to think this wedding thing through, make sure we was doing the right thing. Although, ladies, you'll understand when I say that after that first kiss, I was past being anything but sure.

"Took about four weeks for my dress to arrive through the Wells Fargo, and by then Bill and I'd become right accustomed to the idea of a wedding. So it weren't no problem, once that dress was there, to go right on ahead with the thing.

"We decided to ride Lightning to the church, it being such a fine fall day, and Bill being of the belief that as long as he was riding with me and Lightning, we'd both be just fine. But as soon as I went up on that horse's back, what did he do but buck all over again? This time, though, Bill grabbed for me, which kept me from flying any higher than the church steeple before I came back to earth and bounced, once, on my bustle. The bustle bounce tossed me back up toward Bill, who caught me on the upswing and settled me in the saddle once again. Guess you never know what'll come in handy. He and Lightning must have had a little talk while I was in the sky, because this time, Lightning walked, sedate as an old draft horse, straight on down the road and then right on into the church.

"Seemed like Lightning and me, we'd finally come to an understanding."

❦❦

When Sue comes back to the waiting area, she's jubilant. Not only did she get out there and tell her story, she knows for a fact that Lightning

approved of the telling. He and Toby are standing shoulder to knee on opposite sides of the
tent wall, and they're both nodding their heads.
And the people in the audience? They look
pleased, happy. They're even clapping. For her!
Bill would be so proud.

Sue leans against Lightning, truly relaxed
for the first time since she's come to the market.
Rosey, the last teller, comes by and says, "No
magic there. None at all. Only flying catfish,
talking horses, and love, the biggest magic of
all." She laughs a small laugh. "That was wonderful."

Rosey feels the confidence spell curled up in
her mind, a little something extra just in case.
She looks at Mama Inez, her grandmother, who
nods encouragement. Samson swirls once around
her head and then flies off to wait with Franz and
Roberto. Sue smiles at her, puts her hands on her

shoulders, and turns her toward the telling area. Lightning breathes into her hair, and the next thing she knows, she's sitting on the gold teller's cushion, ready to go.

Rosey and the Wolf

"I'M WALKING THROUGH THE woods on my way to my gram's house, and I'm wearing red. Bright red. Think of just-picked homegrown tomatoes. The heritage kind.

"It's midsummer. The woods are every shade of green you can imagine, and a few other greens as well. Everyone always tells you not to wander alone through the woods, because they all know, for sure, that the head choppers will get you. This is something I've never really believed, but still, head choppers or not, the woods can be a dangerous place. And here I am, decked out in my mother's best red shawl.

"I love this shawl. It's got fringe, and tiny brass bells, and even though I don't need a shawl in the middle of July, I've lifted it and left before anyone knows it's gone. Which just shows that I have no common sense.

"So—here I go to Gram's. Over the river and through the woods, sweating in a stolen shawl dyed the reddest red you've ever seen. I'm like a walking target against all that green.

"And I'm at the midpoint of my trip. The place where, if you decide to go back, it's going to take exactly the same amount of time as it'll take if you just keep moving on ahead. The sun is dappling through the trees, the butterflies are flitting through the wildflowers, a bird even sits on my shoulder. He's a cardinal, bigger than normal, with an orange beak with two yellow stripes. He stays for so long that I give him a name. I call him Samson, and I decide to sing for him. 'The *Golden Vanity*.' It's a tedious kind of song, but there are lots of verses, which keeps your mind occupied. I've hit the point where the cabin boy dives overboard, and all this singing has kept me from digging into Gram's basket, has kept me from adding cookie theft to my sins.

"Singing. Butterflies. Sunshine. Birds. Big man in the center of the path. Which of the above doesn't belong?

"I know, right away. And not only is it a big man, it's Eric Marston, one of the nastiest guys in town. Eric is only a few years older than me, but if they'd kept him in school, he'd be a few years behind me. He works out, but he never works. And he's not just lazy, he's criminally stupid. In and out of the juvenile court system enough that I think he knows all the judges and bailiffs by name. Theft. Breaking and entering. Drinking. I'm almost positive that his last birthday dropped him out of juvie and into adult, so I'm hoping he realizes that assault is a major, go-to-jail kind of thing.

"Ignore him, or say something? I'm sweating, and now it's not just from the heat. I want to take off this dumb red shawl and tie it around my waist, but I'm not about to stop walking, put down my basket, and take time for a little primping.

"'Rosey,' says Eric, and I cringe. Believe me when I tell you it's not what he says, it's how he says it. Like I'm his best friend in the whole wide world. Like we could get cozy and snack on the goodies in Gram's basket, sit under a tree, and have a little party.

"'Hey, Eric,' I say, all business, and I keep on walking.

"He steps in front of me. He moves fast. Predatory. Like a wolf. Samson, startled, flies up to an overhanging branch.

"'Where you going?' he asks.

"I smile, a tight, forced little smile. 'Just across the river.'

"'I could walk with you.'

"'Oh, gee, Eric, you don't need to do that. I mean, you must have something to do that—oh, I don't know. Needs to be done?'

"'Rosey. Don't be silly. You can't walk through here

alone. With that red on, you stand out like a sore thumb.'

"I hate this shawl with a sudden passion. I will never steal it again. I will never steal anything again.

"My inane response to Eric is 'It's my mom's. The shawl.'

"He grins, and now he not only moves like a wolf, he looks like one, too. 'Looks real good on you.'

"'Right. Well, see you, Eric. Got to get going. My gram's waiting for me.' And I speed up my walk. I look like I'm racewalking, and maybe I am. Racing to get as far away from Eric as I can.

"Eric paces me. 'Where's your granny live?'

"'Powton. So, see? I don't have far to go. I'll be just fine.' And I smile that tight little smile again.

"We're almost to the bridge that crosses the Spring-hill River. It's a picturesque, narrow little bridge built more for decoration than transportation, because who's stupid enough to want to walk through the woods to actually get somewhere? But Powton—the edge of it, anyway—is in sight as soon as you get to the top of the bridge. And Gram is on the edge of town. She likes living at the edges of places, my gram.

"Not far.

"Almost there.

"Three feet.

"'Rosey,' Eric says, and he moves fast and blocks the bridge. 'Come on, sit and rest. You're walking real fast. You're all red, you're so hot, moving so fast. Isn't there something to drink in that basket?'

"'No, Eric. I really don't think there is. Excuse me.'

"'Looks real heavy. I can carry it for you.'

"'Not necessary. I'm fine.'

"'Aww, Rosey. I just want to keep you company.'

"When I think of it, it's like a flash of light. A flash I should have had as soon as Eric started to follow me. I put the basket down, off to the side, and stretch my arms a bit. Samson settles back on my shoulder, red on red. 'You know, Eric, you're right. This basket is getting kind of heavy,' and I look at him, waiting.

"As soon as he steps over to his right, steps over to pick up my basket, I hit the bridge, running like my life depends on it. Maybe it does. Samson flies ahead of me, urging me on. Behind me, I hear Eric yelling, 'Rosey! Hey, Rosey! Wait up!' He does not sound happy.

"I do not wait. Up the bridge, down the other side, that's all I need to be safe. My feet slam against the wood of the bridge, slam so hard I raise puffs of dust.

"Eric is behind me. Unbelievably, when I grab a look over my shoulder, I see he's carrying my basket. Now I know what's clinking: the glass jars full of strawberry-rhubarb preserves, canned tomatoes, apricot jam, and Mom's prize-winning garlic dill pickles. What a mess if they break.

"But fast, Rosey, fast. Broken glass is the least of my problems. I pant, my red shawl slips, its bells jangle, and from behind me comes the rattle of jar against jar.

"'Gonna get you, Rosey,' breathes Eric, and he's not even trying to pretend he's my friend, not anymore.

"The curve of the ornamental bridge is higher than I remember. I grab the handrail to help pull myself along, and something digs into my palm. Splinter. Long splinter, and it hurts. I just keep going. Samson wings around my head.

"Almost to the top. Almost have Powton in view. Then, behind me, a change in the rattling. I spare a glance over my shoulder, and I'm just in time to see the thing that might save me. Eric trips, and down goes the basket. Down goes Eric. He's so much closer than I was letting myself believe. I hear him swear as he hits, full length, on his stomach. The bridge quakes. And then, for the whisper of a minute, I feel the tips of his fingers catch on the back of my soft red shoe.

"Just as those fingers start to slip down my heel, I

stomp as hard as a person can stomp while running, and I hear him swear again. Maybe those shoes aren't so soft after all.

"I reach the top of the bridge and see Powton spread out before me. I look back one more time before I start to run down the other side, the side where gravity will work in my favor. Eric is halfway up, on his hands and knees. Won't be long till he's after me again. I do a sprinter's kick, and I go. It's all downhill from here.

"*Bam!* I knock, just once, on Gram's door. When she doesn't answer immediately, I try the knob. Open. I go right on in. By the time Gram comes into her tiny living room, I'm bent double, dragging air into my lungs in hungry gulps. Samson sits on the mantel, his red chest rising and falling with fast bird breaths.

"'Rosey! What's the matter?'

"'Eric Marston'—gasp—'in the woods'—gasp—'following me.'

"'Oh, Rosey. I . . .'

"I wait for the lecture; the never-go-into-the-woods-alone lecture. I wait, and I breathe.

"What I get is 'I'm so sorry. A girl ought to be able to walk in the woods.' Gram sounds angry. But not at me.

"I take my hands off my knees. I breathe more like a regular person now. I look at Gram in disbelief and say, 'You're not going to warn me about the head choppers?'

"Gram snorts. 'Ridiculous. Silly stories for silly children.' She looks straight at me. 'You, Rosey, are not a silly child. You are the kind of person smart enough to know a fairy tale when you hear one.'

"I think of all the times my mother has warned me about the dangers of life. Dangers that she sees everywhere. Believe me when I tell you that 'head choppers' is only the smallest part of her litany. 'Are you sure, absolutely sure, that you're related to my mother?'

"'Positive,' Gram says, and she gives me a grin.

"Gram's door bams again, and this time I know it's not me.

"'Rosey.' Eric's voice is low and growly. 'You forgot your basket.'

"I cover the space between where I'm standing and the door in one balletic leap. The door's just cracking open. I shove against the wood so fast, with so much force, that the damn splinter goes even deeper into my hand. I yelp, but that's all I do. The door slams so hard, the whole cottage shakes. I twist the lock to the right and watch and wait to see what will happen next.

"'Rosey, what are you doing?' Gram says.

"'Keeping him out,' I breathe.

"I don't hear a thing from outside, not now, so I face Gram and say, 'That's Eric Marston,' and it comes out like a low-level wail.

"'Yes,' Gram agrees, 'that's what you said earlier. Now, what's wrong with your hand?'

"'Splinter,' I say, my disbelief even stronger than it

was during the head-chopper exchange. She's worried about my hand while I'm worried about my life? 'But really, Gram. We have more important things to think about.' And I point, my arm straight out, at the door.

"'A splinter can be quite dangerous.'

"'Gram. It's Eric Marston.'

"'I know. Eric isn't the nicest boy in the area. But I have to admit I'm baffled. When you saw Eric, why didn't you just use your protection spell?'

"'Rosey,' says Eric. It's a hoarse whisper that floats through the planks of the door like smoke from a fire. The kind of smoke that lets you know you do not want to open that door, because you can just tell there's a raging inferno on the other side.

"'Gram.' I whisper, too, but it's a much quieter whisper. 'What are you talking about? What protection spell?'

"Gram sighs. 'You don't remember? "Far away, far from me . . ."'

"I stare at her, eyes wide, mouth open. 'That's a protection spell? I thought it was a jump-rope rhyme.'

"My gram looks at me with a why-do-I-bother expression on her face, and I have to agree. How could I not know I carry a protection spell? Just to make sure, I ask, 'Umm, you told me it was a protection spell, right? When you gave it to me?'

"'Yes.' Her voice is clear and sharp to the point of being snappish.

"'Oh.'

"'Rosey.' The door rattles on its hinges.

"'Maybe I should try it.'

"'Perhaps,' Gram agrees.

"'Far away, far from me . . .'

"'Rosey.' Angry. Mean.

"I close my eyes.

"'Or I swear you'll have to flee
and you'll

be gone.

One.

Two.

Three.

Never come to this place again.'

"And just like that, just like magic is supposed to work, the scratches and rattles and whispers stop. Like someone's dropped a blanket over Eric, muffling him, and all the evil he stands for.

"Gram, calm as if she's sitting on the back porch at the end of the world, says, 'That seemed to work. Now let's open the door and get some of that summer air in here. It feels a little stuffy. And then I'll take a look at that splinter.'

"I think, What if Eric's only playing sheep now, instead of wolf?

"'Open the door? Are you sure?' My voice sounds puny.

"When Gram looks at me now, her eyes are sharp as glass. 'Yes. I'm quite sure,' she says, and Samson whistles in agreement.

"I open the door.

"Eric is nowhere. It's as if he's never even been here. But he has, I know. My basket is there, on the stoop, leaking pickles and jam onto Gram's petunias.

"Gram sighs when she sees the mess on her door-step. 'What a waste.'

"'There was bread,' I offer. 'Cinnamon raisin, and it was wrapped in waxed paper. There were scones, too, and cookies. All of that might still be okay.'

"'Lovely,' says Gram, and now she sounds pleased. 'Then I'll just make a pot of tea. And while the water boils, I'll look at your hand.' She's almost to the kitchen when she turns back to look at me. 'And Rosey. You'll remember that spell from now on, won't you?'

"'Oh, yeah. And—well, Gram—you couldn't teach

me any other kind of magic, could you?'

"'I thought you'd never ask.'"

※※

Mama Inez hugs Rosey again when she comes back to the waiting area, and Rosey beams at her. Toby comes over with Samson on his back. The bird settles on Rosey's shoulder as she rubs the big dog's head.

"Gram? Did I do all right?"

"Wonderful, Rosey. Perfect."

※※

Now that the stories are through, Franz and Roberto move their rings around with the speed of master chess players.

"I really think we need three rings for the flying-shoe people," Roberto says, "and we only have the one."

"We didn't know we'd have a trio," Franz agrees. "And even if we don't have three for them, we truly need two for the elf twins."

"We have those extras we made when we were experimenting with that new casting idea. It's just that none of them seem to match up the way that they should."

Franz jingles metal in his hands. Then he grins, a sharp, fast grin, and raises one eyebrow. "Shall we let pure luck decide?"

Roberto looks over his shoulder at Mama Inez. He looks at the tellers, clustered in groups. He checks the spin of the world. And he says simply, "The spin is smooth, the world feels right. Let's give luck its chance."

Franz juggles his handful of rings one more time, then tosses them into the air. As if it were meant to be, three rings fall to the table, two next to B.J.'s and one next to Maddie's. Roberto looks at them with a critical eye and says, "Perfect. Luck must be on our side." Franz matches and counts in his head, then nods in agreement.

Roberto asks, "Now?" and Franz says, "Absolutely now." They walk among the tellers, giving them their memory pieces. The Lizard Man gets a plain, skinny band, something light and almost unnoticeable. Perfect for someone not used to wearing anything on his hands. Renata gets a thick band carved with waves. John is given a gold-and-silver band that tapers on the top and bottom to almost nothing. Earl and Maddie are given rings with carved hearts, Earl's made of brushed silver with the heart on the inside of the ring, Maddie's made of rose gold with delicate hearts circling the band. Rosey gets solid silver, devoid of decoration, that's just big enough for her little finger.

B.J. has a slim band attached to either side of a crescent moon. Wink's is square with rounded corners, and Nodia's is gold with two cat eyes.

Zola's ring is thick and masculine, with one lightning bolt running sideways, all the way around. Sue is given a delicate thing that undulates around her finger like her bucking catfish. And Maisie? Maisie has a band connected by two tiny silver roses.

The tellers are a group now, friends bound by the night's sharing. They laugh and talk and show one another their rings.

But everything ends sometime. People begin to wander into the night. The Lizard Man comes up to Mama Inez and says, "Thank you. This feeling . . . I wish it could last forever," and Mama Inez reaches out and gives him a hug. Zola gives a little bow and a huge grin as he passes them. The elf twins compare their rings and wave excited good-byes to everyone. Wink, B.J., and Nodia call out "Thank you" and leave, arguing amiably. Maisie and Renata leave together, and Maisie is carrying a clean white shell shaped like a trumpet. John spins one more gold coin that Mama Inez catches in midair, and then helps Sue saddle Lightning. Rosey sits in the corner, talking and laughing with Franz and Roberto while Samson does flips above her head. Mama Inez and Toby stand next to each other, holding on to remembered strands of stories and checking the web that holds the spin of the world on the right track.

The market moon begins to fade in the dawn light, and the Serendipity Market folds in on itself like an old, soft tent. Everything and everyone but Toby is gone by the time the sky is the furred pink of a ripe, perfect peach. Even Franz and Roberto have gone back to the house with the witch's-hat roof, taking Rosey and Samson with them. Toby sits in front of the Indwelling, waiting for Mama Inez and watching the sun rise in the stream.

Mama Inez is outside, on the fringe of the entrance to the Indwelling. She looks one last time at the contents of this newest Storie Jar. She moves the bit of lace to the left, and decorates it with the strip of braided red wool. Then she shifts the slipper so it just rests on the river stone from the Mile River. She lifts and polishes the thick, rich gold coin and resettles it beneath the curved ribbon of green brocade, checks that the point of the whorled shell rests just against the lace. Lastly, she runs a gentle finger over the sharpness of the tiny star and settles the golden pea next to it.

When she is through, the jar holds a stylized image of a person, face made of gold, body made of lace, arm of shell, hair of brocade. There is a necklace made of braided tomato-red wool. A foot walks on the world, a world made of stone. In the sky there is a single, sharp-edged star made of crystal, nestled close to a moon made of a smooth golden pea.

Mama Inez stretches, her arms reaching, one at a time, toward the early-morning sun balancing on the horizon. The Storie Jar switches hands twice. Then she crosses the stream and reaches again, this time toward the fading moon.

Her outside ritual complete, she goes into the cool, dim interior. She balances the Storie Jar on the flat black rock on her left, cups her hands, and takes water from the stream. She trickles water over the Storie Jar, one small stream of water for each cardinal direction. The wet jar takes on the color of purple mud and glitters with flecks of mica and gold. While the jar still glitters, Mama Inez again crosses the stream and lights the candle that waits on the white rock on her right. From a plain clay dish next to the candle, she picks an octagonal mirror that winks at her through a single, stray ray of barely-there sunlight. She drips wax from her candle on the top of the jar and gently places the tiny mirror in its wax nest. Then she calls Toby. He comes inside, stepping lightly, and breathes on the Storie Jar, sealing the magic inside.

This new Storie Jar takes its place on the top right-hand shelf, fourth from the left. The mirrors on the filled jars shimmer and shine. Mama Inez curls her fingers into Toby's fur. Together, they walk the circle of the Indwelling. They stop, facing north, south, east, and west, much as they did the day they checked the world's spin and decided they needed this gathering.

From the north they can feel cold, fresh breezes laced with ice. From the south come the scents of blush-pink peaches mixed with glaciers even farther away. Citrus floats in on the air from the west, and there's a rich, salty ocean feel gliding in from the east. Mixed with all of this are the smells of cinnamon and clove, the warmth of new wool, and the rich heat of the rain forests.

Mama Inez and Toby circle again and again, until they're positive that everything is where it's meant to be. Then, each with a breath of ease, of tranquillity, they walk straight out of the Indwelling into the rising sun, and begin a slow climb up the hill to the house with the witch's-hat roof.

Acknowledgments

For getting it started: Vermont College and
the MFA in Writing for Children program

For editing that always made it better:
Jill Santopolo and Melissa Lambrecht

For getting it sold: Erin Murphy

For extraordinary haikus: Leah Key-Ketter

For poetry: Chris Raschka

For the evening star: Maya Anderson

For family: Guy Shuman, Barbara Shuman, David
Shuman, Amy Calkins, Eileen Johnson, Ruth Nichol,
YY Anderson, Ellen Anderson

For encouragement: Sharon Ball, Joy Boysen, Jack Gantos, Jennette Gonzalez, Ashley Gronek, MaryBeth Gronek, Ewelina Lewandowski, Chris Lynch, Bruce Nelson, Melanie Zeck, and the YAs—Aileen, Anna, Katherine, Lucas, Naomi, Nicole, Scott, Tabitha

For everything else: Lance Anderson and Dewis, the best cat ever

EXTRAS

Serendipity
Market

Essay: "MAGIC. AND STORIES."

Newspaper Article: *Huzz Gazette*: Serendipity Market Makes It Worth a Visit to the End of the World

---

A Playlist for *Serendipity Market*

Poem: "How to View the World: Instructions"

Sneak Peek at *Blood & Flowers*

MAGIC. AND STORIES.

Sit by the fire, wrap yourself in your yellow wool blanket, and get ready. What you've just read are stories. Stories about funny things and sad things. Stories that can make you so cold you need to pull that blanket up to your ears. Stories steeped in traditions that go back to early Homo sapiens drawing on cave walls to illustrate their lives.

What you have in your hand is a book of fairy stories. While not even close in age to those cave drawings, they're born out of the same necessity. Someone, somewhere had the need to tell other people the stories that were important, and for years those important stories were found in fairy tales.

Everyone knows fairy tales but after a certain age—6? 10? 13?—they get dismissed as "kid stuff." People who put them in that category are so wrong.

Why? What do these stories do? They can teach (*Little Red Riding Hood*), present family drama (*Cinderella*), or show ways to escape from danger (*Tam Lin*). They can enlighten, and they can entertain. But one of the things they do best is to pull us together by working with all those handed-down tales from so long ago. They're like a collected memory reservoir that we can draw on anytime.

In the late 1600s Charles Perrault published one of the first fairy-tale collections. It held stories like *Sleeping Beauty* and *Cinderella*, tales handed down and down and down. Castles and princesses, glitter and glitz, and danger. Magic was everywhere and everyone knew that magic should never be fully trusted.

But someone did trust this magic. Women and girls. They caught the fairy tales that came their way and pulled them along, passed them on like old lace handkerchiefs. They gathered to sew, to stitch, to knit, and while they worked they talked. What better to talk about than fantastic stories that came from their mothers, their aunts, or original tales that came from themselves?

By the early 1800s, the Brothers Grimm had figured out that the best source for stories (which they saw as a way to preserve their heritage in an age of upheaval) was, surprisingly, their sisters and their sisters' friends. Stand around the corner in just the right spot and listen long enough to the girls chatting and sooner or later you've got a handful of wonderful stuff. Over half of the stories in Grimm came from their sisters' salons.

The Brothers Grimm got it right. They were smart enough to know that the girls understood it *all*—the world, how it worked, and their place in it. Those same girls were able to take that knowledge and talk about it in ways that scared, educated, entertained, and delighted. All the boys had to do was realize how great the things they heard were and write them down.

You're holding a book of fairy tales, and they still work. Not just for girls, either. Male or female, pull your blanket around you, hold your book, and get ready. Read them again. You'll be surprised and thrilled. You'll become brilliant. Just like the Grimm sisters you'll get what you need to know to survive and thrive, all wrapped up in paper made of years and years of stories.

Relax. Enjoy. Get ready to duck. But don't get too nervous.

Remember, they're just fairy tales.

Books I looked at while writing this were:

Clever Maids: The Secret History of the Grimm Fairy Tales by Valerie Paradiz, 2005, Basic Books, New York.

From the Beast to the Blonde: On Fairy Tales and Their Tellers by Marina Warner, 1995, Farrar, Straus and Giroux, New York.

Huzz Gazette

Serendipity Market Makes It Worth a Visit to the End of the World

FN Net News—Located at the end of the world, the Serendipity Market surprises with its eclectic mix of foods and ephemera. Whether you're looking for something obscure, unique, or simply well made, chances are good that you'll find it as you wander and browse along the paths of this outdoor market.

The sellers' stalls themselves are a treat for the eye. Against the backdrop of a pale blue sky and, in the distance, a house with a witch's-hat roof, the retail booths each give off their own brand of magic. Their transitory nature never shows; they present a solid permanence. Their colors—from tangerine to gold, sea blue to new grass green—sing. And their names—The Whistler's Fuge, Sheep in a Shop, Glad

Plaids, Ink and Elegance—make buyers think of poetry.

Wind socks, banners, and flags vie for attention, trying to catch the eyes of buyers. Rainbow swirls and cloud lightning, cartoon chickens and silver chimes, manga graphics and recycled tin stars. Everywhere you look there are sights, sounds, and smells that make you understand why you have senses.

When dusk falls across the top of the house with the witch's-hat roof, music begins to filter in from all directions. Drink sellers exchange lemonades for wine, food becomes more rib-sticking and substantial, and people begin to gather for dancing. Each corner of the market caters to small circles or squares of folk stepping, and eventually everyone is drawn in and out of the main ribbon-drenched dance floor in the exact center of the market.

Then from the west, directly beneath the witch's-hat roof house, come smells of ginger and lemon tea. Bells of all sizes ring from the spangles and fringes of the storytelling tent, and the real work of the market begins. Stories, stories, and more stories.

What I bought at the Serendipity Market

6¾ yards of one-inch-wide sheer gold ribbon for package tying, door decorations, or oddly dressed pigtails.
Where: *Feral Fabrics*

A **floppy purple hat** decorated with a single pale lavender rose to use as an ear warmer, a sun blocker, or a fashion statement.
Where: *Illustrious Caps*

A **large tapestry carpetbag** with rolled handles and a zip top for long journeys into unmapped territories or very large picnics.
Where: *Travelers' Tales*

A **ruby-red glass sun catcher** edged in oranges and the yellow of a freshly picked lemon for dancing sun reflections on the floor, the ceiling, and any blank, bleak wall.
Where: *Blown by the Four Winds*

A **hand-stitched dream catcher** hung with minuscule cowrie shells and the lost feather of a passing junco, for trapping evil dreams that can haunt you when you're not looking.

Where: *Sarah Sleeps*

Seven **organic clementines**; one **pomegranate**; sweet, tangy, **juicy orange globes** with no seeds; and one **hard-skinned love apple** with seeds galore.
Where: *Fruits and Fishes*

A **white bandana** silkscreened with asian-style blue waves rolling toward a starfish beach to use as a neck gaiter, hair tamer, pocket square, or handkerchief.
Where: *Cowboy Clothes*

Beeswax candles shaped like tiny hives for atmosphere, clear air, and peaceful minds.
Where: *Green Lilac Honey*

A **carved snail** that moves when you stroke the wooden ball resting on its back. For use as a worry stone or just for fun.
Where: *It's Only a Game*

Street Food: vegetarian tamales, **hot apple cider** with caramel, **tomato mushroom focaccia**, hand-cut **Belgian fries**, **sugar**

skulls, **dark chocolate truffles**, and **blue-berry tea**.

Where: almost everywhere

Catch Serendipity Market the next time it's at the end of the world. Its eclectic mix of stories, food, and gifts will make you glad you did.

Playlist for *Serendipity Market*

Here are songs that I think represent something about the characters in each story. Listen and see if you agree.

For the book as a whole
    "I Wonder Why the Wonderfalls"
    Andy Partridge
    Theme from *Wonderfalls* TV show

For Mama Inez and Toby
    "Do You Believe in Magic"
    The Lovin' Spoonful
    Do You Believe in Magic

For Roberto and Franz
    "Whittier Boulevard"
    Los Straitjackets
    Rock en Español, Vol. 1

For "The Lizard's Tale"
    "Your Head's Too Big"
    Ditty Bops
    Moon Over the Freeway

For "Conversions"
"Kid"
The Pretenders
The Singles

For "Beanstalks in Enlay"
"Baby Love"
Marah
Let's Cut the Crap and Hook Up Later On Tonight

For "Lost"
"Minor Swing"
Django Reinhardt
Django in Rome 1949–1950

For "Carter House"
"Sweet Jane"
Cowboy Junkies
The Trinity Session

For "The Cabeza River Run"
"Shine on Harvest Moon"
Sarah Harmer and Jason Euringer
Songs for Clem

For "Mattresses"
"Vibrate"
Rufus Wainwright
Want One

For "The Color of Lightning"
"Saginaw, Michigan"
Jimmie Dale Gilmore
Come on Back

For "Rosey and the Wolf"
"The Wolf Is at Your Door"
Howlin' Wolf
Memphis Days: The Definitive Edition, Vol. 2

How to View the World—Instructions

Straddle the moon as you would a horse,
your right leg over, your left leg straight,
and vertebrae by vertebrae
curl your back into the crescent.
Watch for sharp edges.

You may wish to unroll the blanket you've strapped to
your ladder. Remember, you're traveling in space.
It may be chilly.

Watch everything and write it down
in the Moleskine notebook you've brought.
Write legibly.

When sunrise begins to eat the India
ink of night, repeat the steps
in reverse. You may find you need to dangle
from the ladder's second to the last rung.
To ensure landing safety, hold on until
your feet brush the tips of the grass.

For full moons, see Instruction Sheet Two.

Sneak Peek at *Blood & Flowers*

I

"You'll know it when you find it."

$\mathcal{I}$n case you don't know, you use a thin paste of the flour water to stick the poster down. Put them on boards, telephone poles, newspaper boxes—whatever. The paste dries hard, but it's clear and a bitch to get off."

I demoed the process to Lucia and slapped one of our flyers on the wood covering the broken window of Clem's Furniture Store (furniture long, long gone). Then I handed her the paste tub. "Your turn."

Lucia worked carefully, setting her flyer next to mine. A double whammy. The manicured nails on her scarred hands were perfect, cream with ebony tips. Her hands were graceful and when they moved, her scars flared in the just-turning-on streetlights.

She finished and looked over at me. "Persia? How's that?"

I had to make myself stop watching her and look at the side-by-side flyers. I don't know what it is about Lucia. She always makes me wish I were gay. "Perfect," I told her.

Our flyers said:

OUTLAW PUPPET TROUPE

presents

The Bastard and the Beauty

A play of love, dislike, and anticorruption

Place: You'll know it when you find it

Date: Now and then

Time: Eight o'clock, usually. At night.

But things can always change.

Lucia examined her pasted flyer and tapped it with one of those gorgeous nails. "It doesn't say anything about the magic that's in this show."

"You know we never like to draw too much attention to that."

"I know." Lucia nodded. "The anti-fey feelings all

around town. The idea that magic is bad. But people should know that this is good magic."

I made a little hissing noise; then I said, "If we're going to flout convention and get in trouble about magic, why not just put in the whole soap-bubble theory to tell them how the magic gets here in the first place?"

Lucia looked confused. "I don't know the soap-bubble theory. Is it long? Because this is a small flyer."

I raised my eyebrows. "You mean I've never explained my 'how the fey get into our world' theory to you? Wow. I must be slipping."

"You could tell me while we work," she said.

She actually seemed interested. Not many people did, which always surprised me. I thought it was a brilliant theory. I straightened my shoulders, right there in front of Clem's, and pretended I was giving a speech. "Faerie skims around our world like a soap bubble around a glass. When the bubble of us meets one of the bubbles of them, the membranes collapse and the fey can access our world. This only seems to work one way."

"Not always," Lucia said. She spoke in such a quiet voice I almost missed her comment. Almost, but not quite.

I'd forgotten that Lucia wished herself into Faerie once, a long time ago. "So I'm wrong?" I asked. I flushed and added, "You probably know all about this and I probably sound so stupid."

Lucia shook her head. "I don't have any idea about how people go from one side to the other. I don't know how I did it. It just happened, like a sneeze. But your theory makes as much sense as anyone else's."

I blinked three times and said, "You mean I could be right?"

Lucia nodded and I said, "How cool is that? I made it up on my own, you know." I beamed at her.

"It's better than anything I've ever come up with. But back to this." She tapped the flyer one more time. "It might not make people come. We're not telling them about the wonders."

Lucia had a point. I mean, we weren't passing out a lot of information. But there's a reason and it's right there in the name: Outlaw Puppet Troupe. We're obviously not going for mainstream or even politically

18

correct. Social and political commentary is a big part of every production, and there's never a lack of something to say.

We live in a world with lots of problems. The environment is in trouble, the economy's tumbling, and there's crime on the corners and corruption in the capitol. Look back through history and you'll see that these are the kinds of problems that could be problems anywhere, anytime. But here and now, and ever since I can remember, really, the inhabitants of Faerie are blamed for almost everything that goes wrong. Most of that blame starts with our government. I'm not sure why, and I don't remember hearing about it in any history class I ever took. But I know there's antagonism.

I have an antagonism theory, too, to go with my soap-bubble one. It's all about the anti-fey sentiments in our world and where they come from. If I'd given Lucia a speech about that it would have sounded like this: "When you've got plans for power and domination, you need something besides your own activities to occupy people. One of the best ways to occupy people is to give them a common enemy. A good way to identify an enemy is to point out how different they are.

The fey are different—they always have been. Bingo! Adversary right here! Now just throw out some media misinformation and you're on your way. Everyone concentrates on the evilness of the different, and no one has time to pay attention to anything else."

But even though some fey surely are evil, they can't possibly be causing all of the wacky things we deal with on a daily basis. At least I don't think so, but here are samples of the kinds of stories that float around my world.

POINT YOUR FINGER AT THE FEY

Crime? Fey problem. (*Bugle Express*—Faerie Breaks into Shop—Steals Diamonds!)

Failing Neighborhoods? Fey problem. (*Daily Times*—Faerie Landlord Lets Building Collapse! Also—Faerie Gangs Run Rampant!)

Sick environment? Fey problem. (*You and Me Magazine*—Faeries Blow Poison Dust Across Border!)

Drug abuse? Fey problem. (Government Report 2693-6, Paragraph 3 —"It has been noted and corroborated that dangerous drinks and drugs have been coming from Faerie on a regular basis. Citizens are warned to be wary." Or, as Senator Reynolds has said, sounding a lot more nervous—"Danger! Faerie Drinks and Dust on the Rise!")

Total eclipse? Fey problem. (Talk radio WKQS—"Fey stealing life-giving sunshine with magic! Call, starting at midnight with your comments!")

If I had the urge to call WKQS (which I would never have), I'd say I see no problem with magic or with the fey. First, magic is in all of our productions. Sometimes that magic is subtle, and sometimes not so much, but it's always there. And, of course, fey Floss is our chief costumer and puppet guru. If Faerie puppet magic and the sly social jibes we always incorporate don't make us outlaws, then I don't know what would.